THE ENDLESS SHORT STORY

RONALD SUKENICK

FICTION · COLLECTIVE

N E W · Y O R K

First Edition

Library of Congress Cataloging in Publication Data

Sukenick, Ronald.
The endless short story.

I. Title.
PS3569.U33E5   1986   813'.54   84-25960
ISBN 0-914590-94-4
ISBN 0-914590-95-2 (pbk.)

Grateful acknowledgment is made to the following magazines and anthologies in which these stories first appeared: *New Letters* for "What's Watts"; *TriQuarterly* for "Aziff"; *Statements* for "Verticals and Horizontals"; *Lillabulero* for "Fourteen"; *Denver Quarterly* for "Divide"; *Statements 2* for "Dong Wang"; *Criss-Cross Art Communications* for "5 & 10"; *Fiction* for "Boxes"; *Strange Faeces* for "This is the part"; *Formations* for "Duck Tape" and "Bush Fever"; *Black Ice* for "End of Endless Short Story; *Cold Mountain Press Poetry Post Card Series Two* for "Post Card."

Grateful acknowledgment is also made to the University of Colorado Council on Research and Creative Work and the University of Colorado President's Fund for the Humanities.

Published by the Fiction Collective with assistance from the National Endowment for the Arts and the New York State Council on the Arts, and with the cooperation of Brooklyn College, and Teachers & Writers Collaborative.

In addition, this publication is made possible, in part, with public funds from the Greater New York Arts Development Fund, a project of the New York City Department of Cultural Affairs, as administered in Kings County by the Brooklyn Arts and Culture Association, Inc. (BACA).

Typeset by the Institute for Publishing Arts, a non-profit, tax exempt organization funded in part by the National Endowment for the Arts.

Manufactured in the United States of America.

Text design: McPherson & Company
Cover and jacket design: Sara Eisenman
Author photograph: Gregory O. Jones

for Glo

THE ENDLESS
SHORT STORY

to continue   woke up
late   nice people in
this country   drive
toward ignorance   th
e more you know som
ething big   mind lik
e weather   rodia

W   Rodia woke up late that morning. He had a hangover.
H   He was thinking about his red Hudson touring car. His
A   much quoted comment that he wanted to do something in
T   the United States because there are nice people in this
'   country explains nothing. Or if it explains something it is not
S   what it is supposed to explain. This is a documentary. But
W   the problem with it as documentary is that there are not
A   enough facts. And such facts as there are are not the right
T   facts. That is to say they don't explain what you want
T   explained. They explain something else. What you do in
S   such a case is you either explain something else or you ex-
            plain nothing at all but if you explain nothing at all what is the
            sense of writing a documentary? However, that is the trou-
            ble with documentary there are never enough facts. You
            begin with the impression that if you have enough facts you
            can explain everything but in fact each fact you uncover
            requires another fact in explanation so that in a certain large
            sense and I think experience in the exact sciences will bear
            this out the more you know the less you know. Civilization
            then drives toward ignorance you sneer. Nevertheless I
            must answer in the positive. Ignorance in the sense that

Adam was ignorant before the apple. As the fish is ignorant of its water. As the mind is ignorant of its next thought. And perhaps this is the key to Rodia.

An uneducated Italian laborer settles in a then rural area of Los Angeles and working completely by himself for thirty-three years constructs one of America's major art works a series of towers ten stories high. When he is finished he gives the whole thing to a neighbor and disappears apparently to die. These are the hard facts of the story which everyone knows. His name was Sabatino Rodia. Or Simone Rodia. Or Simon Rodilla. Or Sam Rodia. El Italiano. The rural area of Los Angeles became a Mexican section of the city and then became Watts. The more you know the less you know. The facts are a little unstable. There are anecdotes which could imply anything. Here is a snapshot of Rodia thumbing through a book on Gaudi. A little old man at the end of his life he has been persuaded to come to Berkeley and listen to a lecture on his towers. He listens with detached interest. It is as if someone were giving a lecture on his wife who had died years ago before he started the towers. Yes she was beautiful yes he loved her yes he still misses her so what. He once said he wanted to do something big that people would remember him by. When he left the towers he left them to be vandalized by neighborhood kids and torn down by city bureaucrats so what. There were thirty-three years of his life in the towers but now everything was finished. So what so what so what. He did not want to think about his wife. He did not want to think about the towers. He did not want to think about his life being over. They had compared him to Gaudi. At the end of the lecture he asked to see some pictures of the things by Gaudi. "This man," he was supposed to have asked, "he had helpers?" When answered in the affirmative he said, "I never had no help at all."

As I was saying perhaps ignorance is the key. We all of course know what's going to happen next. Only artists don't know what's going to happen next a quirk of ignorance they share with history and the weather. This is the key quirk of the quirky mind that produces the work of the artist. Rodia did not know that day in 1921 that sunny Los Angeles day that he was going to dig a hole in his back yard and bury his beautiful red Hudson touring car. If you had asked him afterward why he did it he wouldn't have known. He didn't do it for a reason. He would have made up a story. It was a story. Stories don't have reasons. Or if they have them they have them after the fact like the weather. Then the reasons become part of the story. The mind is like the weather and this is the reason that everyone likes a good story.

Rodia woke up late that morning. He had a hangover. The Hudson was a seed. A metal seed Rodia planted in his yard. Inside the seed was his whole life up to then. This was the life he was burying. Rodia didn't know his life was a seed. He was conducting a funeral. He was burying his life. One part of his life was over. He woke up late in the morning with a hangover and he knew that part of his life was over. He washed his mouth with a swallow of warm beer and took his spade into the yard. It took him four days to dig the hole and another day to bury the car in it. The following spring the towers began to grow.

the first thing that
happened   savage da
ncing   we hold these
truths jesus-mary   d
ark wings   croo   dar
k soft wings

A   The first thing that happened when I got there was
Z   that I was greeted by a beautiful and intelligent woman who
I   led me into the bedroom and gave me the best blowjob I've
F   had in eight years. That got that out of the way. It was also a
F   promising start for a party. Then the dancing began. We

danced to Jamaican reggae music. Then to Greek bouzouki
music. Then to Spanish flamenco music. Then to Yoruba
drums. Then to Jillala dervish music. We stamped and we
spun we wiggled our asses and stretched our joints snapped
and cracked and jiggled till we were out of our heads. Dizzy.
Blind. Panting like animals. The Parrot retired to a corner.
The Condor woke with a flop of his wings. Where were we.
The dancing had become savage. We were all possibly mad.
If there were knives around we would have torn one another
apart in an excess of passion. The water rose but there was no
channel. Every person present had been provided with an
orgasm on arrival so sex was out. Dissipation was impossible
there was no time. A mood of fear terror even gripped us the
dancing slowed and stopped. We hold these truths to be
self-evident someone began then trailed off. Someone was
mumbling jesus-mary jesus-mary. Then Aziff appeared in a
gout of steam from the radiator. Kin nadho swa he intoned
hand held high index and middle fingers raised and crossed.
Aziff. Ool bagah oon chee la paka ish mool. Aziff. Slee sla slo.
Aziff. Croo. Croo. Aziff. It was as if present company were
excepted. Croo. As if the room became an absence. Croo. As
if it were embraced with dark soft wings. Croo. As if we were
all smoothed and soothed. Croo. It was as if. As if. Aziff.

in the kingdom   went
and   came   a jell of
time and presence t
hick light   scatterin
g cosmos white verti
cals and dark horizo
ntals in the quiet a
ir   coarse texture s
now   in the kingdom
stood up straight we
nt and came

V stand
E up
R straight
T or
I you'll
C grow
A up
L crooked.
S Like the tree. That's what they told him. In the Kingdom.
His tree. In a dirt strip between the sidewalk and the curb
A next to the gutter on the street around the corner before the
N manhole cover across from the garage in front of the yard
D alongside the alley behind the house. That was the King-
dom. Between the curb and the alley. Beyond that
H Neckstore was. And further Down-the-Block and further
O further Next-Block was. And two ways to school up the
R Avenue and by the pickle factory. By the pickle factory was
I the short cut it was actually longer but you came at school by
Z the back through the empty lots and along the cemetery the
O Pecker boy told him how you could ask the pickle men for
N pickles. Everything was very quiet. You ate the pickles at
T eight in the morning on the way to school and they didn't
A make you sick. The Pecker boy lived Neckstore and he
L always knew much more. But that was later. When you lived
S in the Kingdom there was no need for school. Crown Prince
von Mocassin was his name the Kingdom was his claim.
When he was older the Kingdom came. When he stood up
straight. The Kingdom came. And went and came.
The
reason that time seems to be passing more quickly is that the
earth is spinning faster. You have of course noticed how hard
it's getting to jam all you have to do into the day the explana-
tion is simple the days are getting shorter due to gradual
acceleration in the earth's rotation. Last year one already
suspected it but this year there is no doubt. Everybody is
nervous and cranky. Too much to do too little time to do it
every chance you get to look up another week has snapped

by. And not only that the earth is revolving faster around the sun. That probably accounts for the change in the light the light used to be softer clearer now you notice it more am I right. As if the light has been thickening quickening becoming more than a mere medium a jell of time and presence something like that. Of course everything stays in the same proportion there's no feedback from the scientists because it's all relative the same thing is happening throughout the cosmos. Except our psychological clocks deep inside we know it's all wrong we're all suffering from time lag we're never going to catch up not with the whole universe scattering like scared minnows or so the astronomers tell us. Dispersion. Maybe the answer is cosmic saving time a hundred minutes to every hour it would fit right in with the metric system. Or maybe we can scan. Think faster feel more go from one thing to another take it all in at once. All right what's your answer.

The tree. The tree was planted by Queenmother. For Crown Prince von Mocassin. A branch sprouting in a cylinder of chickenwire. There were chickens there then. Not in the Kingdom but Neckstore Pickles Pecker would pull them out of their cages to stroke them and show them off. The light was still and transparent. Crown Prince von Mocassin and Pickles Pecker would go down to the cemetery and stare. White verticals over dark horizontals in the quiet air. Nobody was in a hurry then. Each evening was the end of an era. King and Queen had their faults but they saw to everything. They didn't care about a lot of the things people care about today. Only Queenmother was in a hurry. She cared about a lot of things people didn't care about any more. She was in a hurry about the tree. Crown Prince von Mocassin was the sprouting branch. The Kingdom was coming. Maybe that was why Queenmother was in a hurry about the tree but did you ever see a tree in a hurry? She had no patience when *le peuple* used the young tree for first base in their stickball games. She would break into a demented fury when she saw them pulling and shaking the tree loosening its roots warping the trunk she would spit strings of Yiddish at them out the second floor window shaking her fist. That of course was when it was still possible for old people to yell at kids now they would simply stone her to death on her way to the grocery store. Her arch enemy was Pickles Pecker Crown Prince von Mocassin's best friend. Naturally Crown Prince sided with Pickles even though he and the kids would yell back making fun of the family name von Mocassin what kind of a name was that you couldn't even pronounce it. The fact that it was Crown Prince von Mocassin's tree in a way was Crown Prince made no difference at all.

I. Seymour Hare. There was something dirty about him. He knew about girls. He was older. Crown Prince von Mocassin wasn't supposed to play with him because Stillmore Hare his father liked Hitler. Also he was stupid that was clear even then Crown Prince von Mocassin thought he was stupid because he was older. There is always the possibility that children are little geniuses and it's all down hill from there. The greatest tides of stupidity sweep in with adolescence we never recover. Maybe that explains why I. Seymour Hare was so slow maybe it explains Queen-mother's hurry in any case the tree was growing. Shaky warped and scarred where branches had been torn off during close decisions at first base but still alive. What is this story about? It's about a prince. It's about a tree. It's about standing up straight. It's about a cemetery. It's about a Kingdom coming it's about a Kingdom come. And there's a counterplot involving light and time. You see what's happening here you take a few things that interest you and you begin to make connections. The connections are the important thing they don't exist before you make them. This is THE ENDLESS SHORT STORY. It doesn't matter where you start. You must have faith. Life is whole and continuous whatever the appearances. All this is rather coarse you say that may be but remember coarse is the opposite of slick and the coarser the texture the more it can let in. So. Pussy Hare. The little sister of Seymour Hare. Crown Prince. The Kingdom. Pickles. The cemetery. The tree. Standing up straight. The counterplot involving light and time. Now.

Outbreak of war between the Kingdom and Neckstore. One day Pickles Pecker pulls Crown Prince von Mocassin into the alley. Hey yuh wanna hear a doity joke? he says.

Wha's a doity joke?

You ain't never hoid a doity joke?

Nah.

My fadder tole me it.

Oh. Actually Crown Prince von Mocassin didn't want to hear a dirty joke but there didn't seem to be any way of getting around it. The joke involved a girl from Brooklyn who used the phrase tin bloomers. The punch line was "Whaddya tink my prick is, a can opener?" Crown Prince von Mocassin didn't understand why any girl would want to wear tin bloomers. He didn't understand the joke on Brooklyn accents since they all spoke in Brooklyn accents so what was the joke. And he didn't understand that a prick is in a sense a can opener. He laughed anyway. That was the beginning of it. The next thing was Hey yuh know Pussy Hare?

Yeah.

Yuh wanna see huh bloomuhs?

Wha do I wanna see huh bloomuhs for?

Cause it's doity yuh joik. Crown Prince von Mocassin never remembered exactly what happened after that. Even right after it happened. Even while it was happening. It seems that at that time Pussy Hare was showing boys her bloomers. They called for her and she came over to the alley. Something was happening but Crown Prince von Mocassin wasn't sure what it was. Pussy Hare was lying down and Crown Prince von Mocassin was standing up. Straight. The Kingdom was coming. The Kingdom came. After lunch Crown Prince headed Neckstore. Pickles Pecker was standing in front of his stoop Yuh can't go past he said.

Why not?

Cause yuh joosh. Wham. Pickles lying on his back on the sidewalk Crown Prince didn't even remember hitting him. He went back to his Kingdom.

That happened on a Saturday. The next day was Sunday, December 7, 1941. The day Queenmother had an attack and dispersed. Crown Prince was not at the burial they said he was too young to go to the cemetery. He thought of her as horizontal himself as vertical. Her grave is the subplot of this story. The Kingdom Come. That's when time began to change it started moving faster so fast it got hard to remember things light thickened and congealed in stilted snapshots that left you wondering what happened before and after. By the time the War was over I was thirteen. Bar Mitzvah time. The ceremony was during the winter that night it snowed it started snowing the famous blizzard of 1946. The snow covered Brooklyn it covered Hitler covered the four years of the War the camps it covered everything. Recently I went back. The tree is there the house the house next door the neighborhood all much the same. Still. The people gone. An old house a crooked tree. The glassy surface of a lake beneath which old timbers sway while on the shore faster and faster the kingdom

comes
and
goes
and
comes
and
goes

profound nostalgia m
ass murders total p
romiscuity yearning
s into earnings mot
her dreams and hallu

cinations prunebomb
braunschweigers   in
the depths nothing s
uperficial   g depres
sing concepts negati
ve hallucinations   r
iding wave keeping t
rack making incredib
le distinctions   no
mad nomad

F   to continue   Ricardo awakes from a dream
O   of delighted meditation   he doesn't reme
U   mber the meditation but he remembers the
R   delight   he gets up dresses makes his to
T   ast and coffee haunted by a feeling of p
E   rofound nostalgia   gradually slipping in
E   to the present with its mass murders   se
N   vering all ties with before   yet he rese
       nts it   as compensation he masturbates a
       little before coffee   rewarming some sta
       le fantasies   he tries the one about his
       girlfriend as a prostitute   her name is
       Moonface   he's interested in her because
       of her total promiscuity   at a certain p
       oint he hits on a solution for this prob
       lem   she becomes a prostitute and shares
       her earnings with Ricardo   thus her insa
       tiable cravings are turned to account ye
       earnings into earnings   she of course lov
       es only him she will do anything for him
       even become a prostitute   Ricardo is tou
       ched by her devotion and falls in love w
       ith her all over again   he is also excit
       ed by her new career   her openness her t
       otal availability   her new docility   in co

ntrast with her former betrayals   her so
pping inflamed organ in bed after work
to be honest her degradation also appeal
s to him   her submissiveness   her obedie
nce in fact   at last the ultimate sexual
object   a kind of perfection   almost as
good as a mother   or a slave   rocking ro
cking total needs assuaged a world total
ly responsive   it doesn't work of course
he knows quite well that tigers rage in
her breast   and in his own   each of them
has two tigers a male and a female   each
pair snarls leaps fights until one is de
stroyed   then the victors bloody fangs b
its of flesh and fur clinging to whisker
s set on one another   mass murders resul
t   this severance from the past each morn
ing is also mass murders   still it is be
tter than a dream about a necessary oper
ation to have a plastic throat and assho
le installed   and for which it is implie
d that Ricardo must slit his beautiful n
ew boots down to the bottom   and then on
top of everything else he gets drafted t
oo   what a fix   artificial anus and lar
ynx   boots slit   the train is about to p
ull out for Fort Bilious when Ricardo wa
kes up   the enormous pleasure at hearing
the sound of the waves the rain on the r
oof

    Ricardo lives in a cabin over the s
ea   he goes to visit his neighbor Richar
d who also lives in a cabin over the sea
the difference is the way they deal with
mass murder   Richard is smoking again   h
e's nervous because he's paid into a mas
s murder pool and he's afraid he won't w

in   the winner is determined by the numb
er closest to the tote of victims when t
he mass murder stops   of course nobody k
nows when it's going to stop   also Richa
rd won't reveal his number because he's
afraid someone will steal it   under thes
e circumstances there's very little Rica
rdo can say to reassure Richard   what he
does say is well it's bound to stop some
time   this doesn't console Richard much
how do you know he frets   maybe it will
never stop   besides Richard has other pr
oblems   he has a teacher he won't say wh
o it is   only that he's dead and appears
to Richard in dreams and hallucinations
to give him advice which Richard rarely
understands   and even when he thinks he
does knows his interpretation is only a
matter of opinion   last night Richard's
teacher appeared in his dream with his f
ingers palm outwards spread and joined a
t the tips just in front of his nose and
mouth and told Richard to kiss his finge
rs which Richard did   then he made fun o
f Richard for doing it and removing his
fingers said see they're not even there
anymore   now Richard is angry   he thinks
that is the meaning of his dream   he lig
hts another cigarette goes out and start
s up his little red car   on his way down
to the highway he notices a blond in a sh
ort red dress bending over so that the b
ottoms of her blond buttocks are exposed
on impulse he decides to drive around the
block for another look   maybe Richard wi
ll even ask her to come for a ride   mayb
e she'll even come   Richard knows the de

tour will only take a minute and a half but when he drives around again she's go ne so he turns out on to the highway   up ahead he sees an ominous column of smoke black boiling up into the sky sirens ahe ad and behind   Richard drives for a minu te and a half stops at a traffic jam get s out   flames pour out of an overturned car   a three car accident traffic stalle d up and down the highway   an ambulance pulls away siren screaming   someone they pulled out of a car some say two people they were on fire   they put them out   th e car is just like Richard's little red car   only it's blue

Richard feels bette r today   he goes down to the beach to lo ok for omens   he finds a dead fish some broken shells gulls flying children play ing   the children are beautiful he watch es them awhile   the fish doesn't know th at it's dead the shells don't know that they're broken nor the gulls that they're flying or if they do they don't think ab out it Richard bets   the children don't know that they're beautiful   suppose the y did Richard wonders   would they stop p laying   Richard is envious   he considers as an act of malice telling the children how beautiful they are but he doesn't   t hey'll find out soon enough thinks Richa rd   instead he goes to the bookstore and buys a book   the title is Prunebomb   the first line reads many men master mass mu rder with more mass murder   this is murd er   Richard closes the book   it's alread y evening   he goes to a club where they

have a heavy rock band   he goes dancing
and drinking   he drinks red wine   he dan
ces   the drummer is trying to murder som
eone   he's trying to beat someone's brai
ns out   out into the air like gouts of
fire pulsing through the ceiling murderi
ng Richard's memory   after a while he for
gets about it   he dances   it's a happy m
urder

at the bar Richard meets his friend
Raoul Rouault the artist who lives thous
ands of miles away   Richard is surprised
not so much at the coincidence of meeting
Raoul here as at the fact that he recogn
izes Raoul which he rarely does   the onl
y recognizable thing about Raoul is that
he's always different   sometimes you can
see him change right in front of your ey
es   from all this Richard concludes that
Raoul must be inert   and boy is he right
Raoul has just finished one series and h
as not yet begun another series   he is b
etween series   he always gets inert betw
een series   he always gets constipated t
oo   sometimes Raoul thinks about the eno
rmous turd that must be accumulating in
his gut   he likes to look forward to the
day when it will emerge smooth huge glis
tening with intestinal moistures   Raoul
remembers other such turds from the past
rich brown foot long braunschweigers emi
tted in ecstasies of anal orgasm   he kee
ps a record of them somewhere he'd like
to compare notes with other people espec
ially artists as part of his investigati
on of the creative process   he even has
the impulse to laminate them and hang th

---

em up   sometimes when he's really into a
series he produces one a day on some occ
asions even two   then he wonders where a
ll that shit comes from he can't underst
and it   he doesn't eat a lot   he eats le
ss when he's into a series   in fact it s
eems the less he eats the more he shits
you figure it out   Raoul has stopped try
ing to figure it out   he's started think
ing about doing a series of turds   and h
ow is all this connected with mass murde
r   impossible to say   unless it's true t
hat Raoul feels more like committing mas
s murder when he's most inert which may
be the case   or being mass murdered
                                                    the
fact is that Raoul is here to go scuba di
ving   the next morning he gets up puts o
n his scuba and goes diving   diving is b
y far the best thing for being inert in
Raoul's opinion   the hard thing is to ge
t yourself to make the dive   but once yo
u get down there everything is flowing c
hanging metamorphic   starfish turn into
coral coral turns into flowers flowers t
urn into fish fish turn into your arm e
verything is solemn   a whale sings in th
e distance   in the depths nothing is sil
ly or superficial   not with all that wat
er on top of you   not with the possibili
ty of your death all around you   not wit
h the slow processionals or quick flicki
ngs of the deliberations in the mind of
Triton   at those moments Raoul always fe
els that Triton is in love a love so eno
rmous so complete so inclusive that a ma
n can only sense it through the echo of

its great throb that pulses in his achin
g chest   when this happens Raoul knows i
t's time to return to the surface   the t
rick is to take the depths back with you
Raoul knows that men must live on surfac
es and that for us depths have to become
surfaces   or else   when Raoul takes off
his diving mask he's unrecognizable and
ready for another series   this series is
about a character called Ricardo   Ricard
o is worried about mass murder   he wants
to know what to do about it how to avoid
it   once he heard about an intelligent a
ttractive young woman who had leukemia
every year she had to go and have her bl
ood completely changed   all of her own b
lood siphoned off her body completely fi
lled with new blood   in this way she cou
ld continue her life very adequately   bu
t only for a few years she didn't know h
ow many   what did this have to do with m
ass murder   Ricardo didn't know   it was
one of the things that interrupted his m
editation on the subject his drive towar
d a solution   or maybe it was part of th
e problem that was worth thinking about

                                          s
ex was another interruption   he would be
concentrating all his faculties on mass
murder and suddenly he would be thinking
about tits stiff cocks round asses cunts
like ripe melons women he desired women
he didn't even know he desired someone h
e saw in the street that day   grunting g
utgrinding   orgiastic   gritty fleshgrabbin
g groundfloor jungles of sex   I mean rea
lly basic stuff   for Ricardo the letter

16

g was the magic letter of sex   enormous
erotic reverberations   he once knew a gi
rl named Gigi   she drove him gaga   his f
avorite french dish was gigot   listening
to jug bands threw his whole body into a
kind of sexual jig jerking and jumping l
ike the palsy   he loved jam also jelly
soft g's were subtler than hard g's he l
oved both   soft g's were insinuations ov
er cocktails a secret sinuous touch unde
r the table   hard g's were later in bed
cursing grabbing grunting begging shitea
ting hardcore fuck   Ricardo wondered whe
re all this stood in relation to mass mu
rder   maybe it was part of the solution
or maybe it was part of the problem   par
t of the problem was changing   by that R
icardo meant that he found himself chang
ing all the time and he couldn't keep up
this led him to the idea that part of th
e solution was also changing   maybe the
whole problem was changing maybe mass mu
rder was changing all the time so that R
icardo would never catch up   one of Rica
rdo's mottos was if you can't catch up c
atch on   by this he meant that maybe you
could find a way of changing that would
keep up with the changes around you and
in you   maybe if you could ride the brea
king wave just right the wave would neve
r break   that was another of Ricardo's m
ottos
        another interruption was fame   wh
enever Ricardo starts thinking about fam
e he can't think about anything else   fa
me is blinding   it's the flash of an exp
losion that prevents you from seeing any

thing else   and once the famebomb explod
es nobody can put it back together again
or you   in quite the same way   being fam
ous is like finding the girl you were fu
cking last year on the cover of a magazi
ne   he imagines it as a kind of unpleasa
nt orgasm with a selfish woman   the exer
cise of a certain muscle that had to be
exercised but that would leave him feeli
ng used and unsatisfied   when absorbed i
n these distracting thoughts Ricardo can
see very little beyond them   this is the
nature of distraction that hides from us
so much of our experience   it's like hav
ing a negative hallucination Ricardo thi
nks to himself   you can't see something
that's really there   the concept of nega
tive hallucination fascinates Ricardo s
ometimes he thinks that his whole life i
s a negative hallucination   how depressi
ng   how depressing to have a concept abo
ut it   like all of Ricardo's concepts th
is one is another distraction   forget co
ncepts what Ricardo needs is concentrati
on   Ricardo knows this very well himself
it's like when you get up in the morning
and there's nothing but fog   you don't w
ant an idea about the fog   turning on th
e radio and hearing the weather report t
ell you it's foggy and why   you want to
flow into the fog so that it fills you
you want to notice shadows emerging   sil
houettes   shapes   you want to notice the
rainy sea smell the shiftings of texture
so that this insupportable blanket of in
ertia becomes a blank of potential   an e
xpectancy   till out of your concentratio

18

n and the day's come hummingbirds and mo
ckingbirds   and between the songlike fli
ght of the one and the flightlike song o
f the other the fog lifts in your eyes
light floods in   Ricardo will be getting
somewhere he thinks if he knows when he
is having a negative hallucination
                                          and
now a personal message from Richard   Ric
hard wants to confess something   he has
a phobia   his phobia is fear of death   R
ichard is afraid that he's going to die
one day   he is afraid that something is
going to come through his chest and pier
ce his heart   or that his intestines wil
l start bleeding and never stop shitting
all his blood out his ass   the very thou
ght of it makes him scream   Richard feel
s that the only defense against this dea
th is having an erection   he feels that
as long as he's having an erection he ca
n fend it off   if his cock comes up he k
nows he's alive   he has a weapon a staff
of life to beat off death   when Richard
feels this way he starts beating off   Ri
chard knows he is deeply neurotic   but he
also feels that life itself is deeply ne
urotic   what worries him is whether he ha
s the right neurosis or not   wouldn't it
be better in the long run if his neurosi
s centered around money   or power   or wo
uldn't it be even better maybe if his ne
urosis focused on kindness gentleness
spreading good feeling making everybody
feel really great   that's the kind of th
ing the world really needs in Richard's
opinion   is Richard right

19

Richard goes to
meet Porfessor Sukenick   he wants to ask P
orfessor Sukenick about all this stuff
there is a book that explains everything
says Porfessor Sukenick   but it hasn't y
et been written   actually it is being wr
itten right now   but it will never be fi
nished   it is being written by you and m
e and everybody and it includes almost e
verything   it's called Prunebomb   what i
t does not include is what interests me
as soon as I discover what it does not i
nclude I include it   then it doesn't int
erest me anymore   in my opinion that's t
he best way to go about things although
certainly different folks have different
strokes   and to tell the truth about thi
s book that explains everything and that
will never be finished it explains very
little   maybe it explains nothing   in fa
ct the moral of that book   if any   runs
against the necessity or even the profit
of explanations   this book that is alway
s being written is simply a way of keepi
ng track because it's always important to
know where you are   but what does that e
xplain   if I discover that I am taking a
ride on the Cyclone in Steeplechase the
Funnyplace does that explain anything   o
bviously it raises more questions than i
t yields answers   if you want answers ge
t in touch with Uncle Don   Uncle Don is
Richard's dead guru   he's an answer man
Uncle Don is full of answers   here are s
ome of them   it's behind the radio   the
square root of seven   Helena   Maxine Pat
ty and Laverne   Petrarch   a fat oranguta

ng   a garbage truck   the Dutchess of Mal
fi   no trespassing   of course you will
want to know what has all this to do wit
h mass murder   that is a question I try
to answer in my lecture An Illustrated T
alk By Porfessor Sukenick

as Porfessor
Sukenick talks he's gradually being surr
ounded by magnificent snails   slow majes
tic movements   ocean liners of the lawn
shells like sails   Porfessor Sukenick do
esn't notice these magnificent creatures
in their glistening khaki sensitive hor
ns waving making incredible distinctions
among subliminal modulations coming from
the earth   their shells are like ears   h
e doesn't notice those coming in from th
e garden nor the one kissing the glass o
f the window with its foot   Porfessor Su
kenick talks and talks   the snails gathe
r   they're not all that slow either I me
an they're not jackrabbits but still   at
this exact instant on Rue Monsieur le Pr
ince in Paris Claude Balls the existenti
alist critic and I. Bitchakokoff the mar
xist theorist pass one another without r
ealizing it not knowing they have the sa
me destination nor that it has anything
to do with snails   if Porfessor Sukenick
were to think about that encounter at th
is moment it would only make him reflect
on his own European origins   yet to say
origins in Porfessor Sukenick's case wou
ld be to say too much   for Porfessor Suk
enick was of the race of Nomads that irr
itating brilliant strain of humanity hea
vy with fate whose generations wander ov

er the map of the earth bringing civiliz
ation   and its tristesse   something tear
s loose in Porfessor's head   it is his i
ntermittent or should we say by now habi
tual rebellion against being a Nomad whi
ch distinguishes him from other Nomads
his rebellion against that enormous burd
en of Nomads the bloodsworn responsibility o
f not going mad   this time the rebellion
takes the form of an appearance of his d
ouble   even before he appeared Porfessor
had intuited his double so that the appa
rition though not a surprise was neverth
eless a shock   he called himself Rossefr
op Kcinekus and the revelation he brough
t was his discomfort with the ground tol
d by the constant shiftings of his feet
from one side to the other and by the tw
itchings of his body   a man who would ne
ver find his place   never   that is why P
orfessor Sukenick has so much to learn f
rom snails   once a year at the vernal eq
uinox the earth grants a boon to one ind
ividual   nobody knows the criteria   this
year the individual is Porfessor Sukenic
k   the boon is snails   the lesson is the
ir intimacy with the earth   Porfessor Suk
enick doesn't know this yet   less so Cla
ude Balls and I. Bitchakokoff
                                at this
time Porfessor Sukenick is possessed
by devils   it is their peculiar characte
ristic that they only possess one part of
his body at a time however they jump aro
und a lot   their recent possessions have
included Porfessor's eyes his lower back
his teeth and his asshole   currently the

y're concentrating on his chest   they're
into his chest like Peter Pain   remember
him   it's almost enough to make Porfesso
r Sukenick write in to Uncle Don   in fac
t he does write in to Uncle Don but rece
ives the same answer he always gets from
him   that is it's behind the radio   Porf
essor Sukenick always looks behind the r
adio but it's never there   shit   in fact
the devils are Balls and Bitchakokoff   t
he snails are filling the room   Balls an
d Bitchakokoff are moving in   Porfessor
can hardly make a move now without crush
ing a snail which then begins to rot and
smell awful   he had to do something   Bit
chakokoff with his vicious illusions abo
ut social reality and Balls with his pre
tentious allegories of meaning   and now
up out of the compost heap rises Uncle D
on   covered with mulch and snails algae
runs out of his nose moss molders in his
ears   there's murder in his eye   they te
ar you apart to tell you what's wrong he
screams   they tear you apart to tell you
what's wrong and what's wrong is that yo
u're torn apart   and then they have the
nerve to stand there and tell you how if
you change everything is going to get be
tter   what to do and why   but it's not g
oing to get better   it's going to get wo
rse whether you change or not   it's go
ing to end in mass murders   it always ha
s   it's going on right now   and there's
nothing to do this story is postponed   t
here is a fire in this story   please wal
k to the nearest exit   scram   beat it   g
et out   ciaou   au revoir   hasta la vista

23

blah blah blah says Balls   blah blah bla
h says Bitchakokoff   blah blah blah they
say blah blah blah blah blah blah blah b
lah blah blah blah blah blah blah blah b
lah blah blah blah blah blah blah blah b
lah blah blah blah blah blah blah blah b
loh bloh bloh bloh bloh bloh bloh bloh b
loh bloh bloh bloh bloh bloh bloh bloh b
loh bloh bloh bloh bloh bloh bloh bloh b
leh bleh bleh bleh bleh bleh bleh bleh b
leh bleh bleh bleh bleh bleh bleh bleh b
leh bleh bleh bleh bleh bleh bleh bleh b
lih blih blih blih blih blih blih blih b
lih blih blih blih blih blih blih blih b
lih blih blih blih blih blih blih blih b
luh bluh bluh bluh bluh bluh bluh bluh b
luh bluh bluh bluh bluh bluh bluh bluh b
luh bluh bluh bluh bluh bluh bluh bluh b
luh bluh bluh bluh blook out it's going to
explode

absurd   intelligence
secret code   occult
murky data out here
harder getting down
than   being watch
ed being followed dr
owned voices absolut
e shock men can't d
o that   lethal teleol
ogy

D
I
V
I
D
E

It began when the C.I.A. contacted my publisher and asked for a copy of my last novel. At first I thought it was funny. What would the C.I.A. do with an off-beat novel that even most of the critics couldn't understand? I was flattered, in a way, for the attention. I asked the publisher if they were sure it wasn't the International Communications Agency, the I.C.A., which runs international cultural events for the government. No, it was the C.I.A., and the publisher hadn't sent the book because they hadn't sent payment for it. I thought I might send them a signed copy, compliments of the author, with a jocular dedication. "Flattered that you find my work Central, Yours..."; "From one who also works for the Intelligence, Fraternally..."; "We are all Agents, Subversively..."

Then suddenly it wasn't so funny. Absurd, perhaps. Inexplicable. Maybe somebody up there with a literary bent heard about the book by word-of-mouth and just wanted a freebie, pure literary curiosity. Gordon Liddy, maybe? While it was true that the President had just authorized the C.I.A. to engage in domestic intelligence again, I couldn't believe that included literary intelligence. Maybe they'd concluded my novel is a secret code. I mean, my work is not for everyone. Still who knows what might be considered political these days? Possibly the very fact my work is not for everyone was considered political. Maybe I was considered an "elitist." Maybe, for all I knew, they liked the fact that I was an elitist. Maybe they were going to try to recruit me. Didn't the very fact that they neglected to include payment with their book order imply a certain complicity, as if they could expect everybody's cooperation?

Expect cooperation. That, on the other hand, seemed a little menacing. Nonsense, I was just letting my imagination run on. But what did they expect? What did they think an imaginative writer was going to do with this kind of occult event? Forget about it? The C.I.A. asks for one of your books just like that, for no reason at all, and you're supposed to forget about it? Or maybe I wasn't supposed to forget about it. Maybe I was doing just what they wanted me to do. Get paranoid. Be aware they had their eye on me. Involve myself in endless speculation about their motives. Maybe I'm in effect collaborating with them already, despite myself and without knowing it. It is not totally impossible that the whole point of all this is to get me to write C.I.A. stories. And what would be their motive for that? Why, to help make everyone aware of their presence of course, but in a subtle, oblique way, nothing heavy handed or threatening, nothing to chill the atmosphere, just a quiet reminder that they are there, invisible, occult, omnipotent, there.

But of course, this is all ridiculous. The whole incident—is it an "incident" already?—is no doubt completely innocent. I was making molehills out of goose bumps. The C.I.A. has a right to read novels too, just like any other citizen. And any citizen has the right to express suspicion. Who could be that suspicious of me, I wondered. And for what, since I am completely innocent. Innocent? Of what? Who mentioned anything about being guilty of something? That's not even a consideration. Surely the message implied in this affair, if there is a message and it is an affair, is nothing more serious than "Be careful," a warning that could be considered as much a favor as a threat. Thanks.

I understood very well what was happening to me. As usual my imagination had seized on the murky data of experience and had made of it a continuation of my writing. But understanding it didn't necessarily mean I could do anything about it. My life was an endless short story whose episodes derived as much from the unpredictable currents of my mind as from the dark flood of experience. The best cure for this mood was sunshine, especially the hard clear Colorado sunlight shining outside which did not permit the ambiguities of chiaroscuro to obscure the sharp snowpeaks of the Continental Divide that I could see from my window, fourteen thousand feet of pure fact sawing into the steel blue sky.

I put on my down jacket and walked to a trailhead at the edge of town. From there it was a short, steep hike up through a deep slot into the first pinnacles of the Rockies to a high rampart that gave a clear, far view of both the jagged line of the Front Range and the Great Plains receding sixty miles into the blue distance in the direction of Chicago. Perspective. It was one of the virtues of living on the Divide. Perspective and schizophrenia. The shopping plazas at the east side of town were populated by heavy, dish faced farmers and grey suited businessmen, while the bars on the western edge had a clientele of mountain men with fleas in their beards, local cowboys in down vests and hip bachelors with styled hair and clothes like Southern California. But the geography here suited me, on the blade edge of America. Having been raised in New York and having lived a long time in California, it seemed just right that I should end up on the Continental Divide. When I lived in New York I used to feel paranoid about the unleashed libido of California and when I lived in California I used to feel persecuted by the grey power centers of the east. Now I could look in both directions and by a slight shift in sensibility or location feel part of either. The best cure for paranoia is schizophrenia.

Somewhere between my cowboy boots and my Brooklyn head I had made my accommodation to the Sun Belt. In my mind, by moving to the Southwest I had finally become an American. New York was not America, it was New York, and in Los Angeles it was easy to see oneself as the offspring of immigrants finally arrived in the promised land, cosmopolite in utopia. But as in Paris when your interior monologue imperceptibly switches to French, out here —I could still think of it as "out here" —I was beginning to catch myself thinking in Cowboy: "A short ways up the trail here an ah kin see the tall buildins in Dinver." And I could, from a distance of thirty miles horizontal and a half a mile vertical, which always gave me a small shock since, where I came from, you looked from the tall buildings down at everything else, not down from anything else at the tall buildings. Yup, out here I had finally become one of us, spelled U.S. That is, until this casual gesture by the C.I.A. —if the C.I.A. made any casual gestures—placed the edge of the wedge in the fault of my contained schizophrenia, the fault being an old paranoia native to the alien coasts. The Americans are after me again.

I was on a pinnacle just under the crest of the first wall of the mountains, the Divide stretching from my view north to Wyoming. Way down below I saw the town pooling in a bowl of the plains, the red sandstone and green grass of the campus and, with my binoculars, I could pick out my house. On a mesa rising out of the plains beyond a low line of hills I could look down at the modernist castle of the National Center for Atmospheric Research and, ten miles south, on the next mesa over, at the neat metallic spread of the Rocky Flats nuclear plant where all the plutonium triggers for all the atom bombs in America are produced. People who bought houses around here had to sign a statement that they knew they were living in a ten mile radius of Rocky Flats. There was a town downwind whose water supply had been contaminated by radioactivity.

But radioactivity was not what I thought about when I thought about Rocky Flats, and here comes my paranoia again, what I thought about was the last war, and by the last war I meant the next one, and the certainty that one of the first Russian bombs to drop would drop on Rocky Flats and goodbye. That was a circumstance that had its advantages as well as its disadvantages though, and here comes schizophrenia to the rescue, since if it meant that folks around here would be among the first to go, who would want to be around afterward anyway? Nevertheless, there was a bumper sticker popular in the area that read, "Close Rocky Flats As A Nuclear Bomb Plant," and there was usually more than one demonstration a year at the plant, often including civil disobedience, with attendance at times numbering in the tens of thousands. One of these I had myself attended.

Did they know? Was that it? Did they know, for that matter, that I sometimes came up here and sometimes trained my binoculars on the place?

But I was tired of thinking about Rocky Flats. I had come up here to get away from all that. From my pinnacle there was a narrow ridge slicing off behind me toward the higher cliffs. When I say narrow I mean a razor edge of about a foot of rock with an occasional stunted pine growing out of it and a straight drop of about five hundred feet on either side. I had never tried walking across it and I knew I shouldn't but I decided to anyway. One of the problems of climbing around in the mountains is that I tend to get over-exhilarated by the altitude. It's a physiological effect of the thinning air, like getting drunk. The higher you get the higher you get. I find myself doing things that my better judgment tells me I should never do alone, leaping from rock to rock like a goat in places where any slight accident that prevented me from getting back down out of the mountains would mean death by exposure. But I wanted to escape my fears of civilization. I prefer fear of nature. I figure I can make it across the ridge if I'm real careful, go slow and use hand holds at the scarier parts. On the other side I can see a break in the cliff through which it looks like I can climb all the way to the crest. From there I might be able to get a glimpse of the family of golden eagles I had seen above the peaks once, playing in the updrafts.

I start picking my way along the ridge trying not to look down the sides of the drop, looking down makes me feel like my rectum is falling out. I'm sure that if I can get across here safely I'll be able to get back down the same way. I don't know much about rock climbing but I know one thing they say is that it's always harder to get down than to get up. Several people a year get stranded up here, sometimes because of a sudden change in the weather, which happens frequently, and some just because they find it's a lot harder to get down. Some try, some die. Some stay put and are gotten out by the local mountain rescue team if their absence is discovered before they freeze to death, which can happen in a few hours, depending on the weather, and if they can be located. Some are found years later, their skeletons matched up with the missing persons roster by their bridgework. Half way up the incline of the ridge I stop to rest. It's steeper than I thought and my heart is pounding from the exertion and the altitude. Behind me now the plains and mesas are out of sight, all I can see are the pine covered foothills.

I hear a slight thrashing noise and in the ravine below me I discover a mule deer making its way through the trees. I get my binos on it, a pretty good sized buck working its antlers through the dense pine branches. For a moment it seems trapped, then shaking its head violently, breaks free and disappears down a gully. At that moment, following the abrupt movement of the deer with my binos, I become disoriented, and trying to refocus as I drop the binos from my eyes, get dizzy, lose my balance, and start an odd dance on my rock perch that seems to take place in slow motion as I try to prevent myself from falling. Falling. Then fall, for an instant totally out of control, to land just below my rock on a patch of dirt at the edge of the big drop, safe but nearly blanking out, and with the bizarre sensation that someone is watching me. Who?

The thought fills my mind for a fraction of a second, then evaporates. Someone watching me? I put it down to altitude inebriation, get up carefully, take a few deep breaths and head on up the spine of the ridge. From here on it rose at a steep angle, and though I practically have to crawl up the last fourth of its length I make it across without further trouble. But when I stop to look back from the other side I'm amazed at what I just climbed. The ridge seems to drop off into space and disappear like the tip of a knife. Up ahead, though, it still looks like I can make it through the cliffs to the top. Except I would have to hurry, because it's getting a little late in the day.

Behind the first cliff the way opens out unexpectedly

into a wide snowy field, still sloped steeply, but that allows me to climb much faster. Here again, even though I can see for quite a distance behind me, I have the feeling of being watched, even followed. It puzzles me, I'm already frightened of the mountains and it raises the level of dread like water filling a sink. Irrationally, it makes me climb faster than I should to conserve my energy, panting up toward the opening in the next line of cliffs. I reach a kind of steep gully and begin scrambling up over icy boulders, realizing I'm not wearing the right shoes for this kind of climbing, I have on boots, but not cleated hiking boots. Am I trying to get away? And if so, from what? Then all at once I understand that to be followed I don't have to be followed by somebody. Or something. It's utterly possible just to be followed, as simple as that. By what? By nothing, or by everything. Just to have the experience of being followed and, correspondingly, the impulse to escape, to get away, and why not? I recognize for the first time that it's not only me, that everyone is followed, that it has become the fundamental condition of our lives, that we think we are being followed by this agent, or that organization, or such and such bureaucracy, while the fact is we are being followed by history itself in the form of various agencies but sometimes more diffusely as a huge, pervasive presence, like a terminal disease, like a mass grave, like drowned voices, like that genre of absolute shock beyond pity of which we must speak but about which there is nothing to say.

I'm climbing a kind of chimney now where the gully has narrowed to a steep ascent of about sixty degrees. The sky has greyed over and it's getting cold. I'm not wearing warm enough clothing for this kind of weather. Reaching the top of the chimney in a state of extreme fatigue and chill, I look around for some kind of shelter. I had heard about the dangers of hypothermia and know I should have brought something to eat. I'm on an immense, up-tilted rock shelf, bare of trees or bushes. From there I can see it's begun to snow on the peaks to the north like heavy grey curtains descending from a grey sky. I know that as soon as it starts snowing here it's going to be impossible to get down. As I start climbing toward the ridge, hoping for a cave, the wind starts gusting, and before I have a chance even to arrive at the top it begins to snow. I settle behind some boulders to wait out the blinding, wind driven storm, but even from the shelter of the rocks it's impossible to see. The air is a white sheet, a blank page. And it's freezing. Nothing could survive in this kind of environment, I think, not even the animals. They had been happy at first in the preserve, or so we thought, but it soon became ambiguous as to whether the barbed wire was meant to keep them out or us in, or even as to who was "us" and who was "them." We thought of us as ourselves and the animals, living together inside, but we could get out and the animals couldn't. Outside they had weapons and some kind of vague, lethal teleology. There was mounting pressure on us to leave. We were given assurances that the animals would be taken care of, and so finally we left. But stories began to filter out, like the instant slaughter of whole herds of elephants with automatic weapons and anti-tank rockets. And so we came back. We found the animals starving and diseased, penned up in an ever smaller perimeter of barbed wire, and yet the wire was their only defense against even greater obscenity. We resolved then to stay and do all we could to protect and save the preserve. The animals were upset but still innocent, nevertheless our supporters gradually dropped away and deserted us. They came at the moment we were stripped of support. They had tanks and troop carriers. They cut the barbed wire. The animals looked on, wide-eyed, apprehensive, numb, a rhino, two hippos, something with fluted horns, the cats hiding in the bush. We jumped into the muddy gap through the wire, blocking the way. Nobody is going to come through here, we said, taking our stand in the mud. We were nude. There were three of us, our bodies cut and scarred. We knew what they wanted to do and we told them they weren't going to do it. Because, we said, men can't do that. We repeated this three times. Then the dream panned across our three pale, rigid bodies. Each of us, one with a stump, one with a lumpy scar, one with a jagged incision, had had his penis cut off.

another trip   curve
of earth making conn
ections finding style
alarming white stuff
focus unfocus   the b
inos the rhinos   eye
s go blind brain gra
nulated by time   daw
n buck leaping   more
attuned to energies
than comprehensions
sleepwalking through
the big picture   lon
g duck   ten geek

D
O
N
G

W
A
N
G

He was glad to be back from his trip. But as soon as he said it he realized that being back was just the beginning of another trip. So where did that leave him? From where he sat he could see the curvature of the earth, just as he could from the plane, from where he sat way up in the mountains, overlooking the plains. He could see the horizon curving, very slightly, maybe forty miles away from where he sat, through a cleft in the mountains. He was making connections, as usual. He was trying to make connections between one trip and another, among trips, trips past and trips to come. He was starting off on still another trip, the connections trip. He liked making connections. He liked making connections because it slowed him down. It slowed him down and it made him feel connected. He didn't know if it was better to feel connected, but it made him feel better.

But connected to what? Connected to other connections, he supposed. Alarming white stuff. What is that connected with? This might be good to read, he would read it aloud some time to try it out, the cadences seemed right. He had trouble reading. He'd always had trouble reading, even not aloud and to himself. When he was young reading was not allowed, not in bed, not late at night, late into the night when he wanted to read. Maybe the trouble was that he wanted to read but he didn't want to read in straight lines, he wanted to read two or three lines alternately, simultaneously, in his own order not the order that was already there in the straight lines. It takes years to find a style and once you find it you go on to something else or else you're lost. Finding your style is like being back from a trip, it's just the beginning of another trip. In any case, this was what he found, he found the way he wanted to read, or be read, and finally he would do it.

                                        brain granulated by
time   covered by alarming white stuff
        old Juanitito   tomorrow he would see Dong Wang
back from the long voyage   after
                    labor day weekend   the word for today
            clouds snow fog   snert
        forty miles of plains
                                focus unfocus
            the binos   the rhinos
turn in the dust   second baseman turns throws
                    focus unfocus
                                making the sound snert
from this distance   Dong Wang snorts
                    hocus pocus   in his cave
        cuevas cuevas   montanas   eyes go blind
irregular   never   no rules
                focus   unfocus   new focus
                                old Juanitito, a tiny old
man, blind, alarming white stuff filmed his eyes. He lived in
a two room cabin in the mountains, the back room was actu-

ally built into a natural cave, there aren't many here, granite, as opposed to limestone of Sierras. He lived up at 8,000 feet, that cave came in handy in five feet of snow or when the Chinook started blowing at 100 mph. There was nothing special he wanted to ask the old man, he just felt drawn up there, and that's the kind of feeling you learn not to ignore when you live here, in the montanas, in the southwest, in the emptiness, in the power center of the country. Crazy talk for a kid from Brooklyn, n'est-ce pas? The visits were ritualized in their way. The old man was always there, never surprised to find him at the door. Shake hands, sit for a cup of coffee, talk about the weather in broken English, broken Spanish. Frankly, he sometimes wondered whether the old man was all there. In a way he undoubtedly wasn't, absent minded etc., brain granulated by time, talk disconnected. But in another way he just as undoubtedly was. Let's say there was an energy field he created, like sitting in an orgone box but not really, but some kind of energy, frightening at the edges, like you would skid skid skid off into something very weird, but basically benign, he had done the old man a good turn once, that counts make no mistake, if it weren't for that he wouldn't come. The old man wasn't all there, but whatever part of him wasn't there was definitely somewhere else. Where? Nothing happened. They talked. He left. And he realized he felt very different. Maybe it was this, that the things that had seemed important before were suddenly muted, buried under sand, under snow which he now skiied across, the contours of the land very different from before the storm, the crucial landmarks changed, the feel of the landscape. There's a place there, on the ski trail, where you can see the skyscrapers of Denver, just make them out, tiny, below, and if you use your binos you can see a minute airport with microscopic jumbo jets taking off and landing. The inertial motion of his life suddenly altered, an abrupt turn, some heavy animal skidding in the dust, a sound like snert, a redirection of forces. Let's say it comes to this, that things that once seemed important no longer seemed quite so important, and things he used to ignore he could no longer ignore. All those crazy little feelings, do this now, don't do that now, tuned out by the static and different energy of the city, that was the insane, magic way his life now began to organize itself. He became a sleepwalker.

ten-geek
sun bleeds up from horizon
dawn buck leaping

He found a new voice. A new sleepwalker voice. At dawn he took a new name, Dawn-buck-leaping. A new ten-geek name.

Dawn-buck-leaping, ten-geek sleepwalker, went down the mountain. He went to see his fat friend Madame Lazonga. Madame Lazonga was a sleepwalker, also she gave rubs. She was known locally as a rubber, that's how she made a living, but Dawn-buck-leaping also knew she was a sleepwalker. He wanted to ask her some questions about sleepwalking.

These mountains are magic, she explained. They go up and down. Since they go up and down the people who live in them also go up and down. It's partly the thin air, you have to breathe deeper in, deeper out, it affects the blood, everything is intensified, higher is higher and lower is lower and in between is more in between. It's a question of the flux of energies. In the mountains we become sleepwalkers, more attuned to energies than to comprehensions, like the animals. In the mountains there are many energies. The energy of the cosmic rays stream through you, the energy of the granite irradiates you, the push and pull of the moon, the lucid confusions of the stars. Watch out. In the mountains men jump off high cliffs out of exhilaration and women through despair are driven to erotic frenzy. One day you will wake up, but the reality you waken to will seem different, what was formerly reality will seem like another dream, a dream among dreams, and nothing will ever be the same.

What is ten-geek? asks Dawn-buck-leaping.

Ten-geek means everything is raised to the

tenth power. Or lowered. Tenth is an exaggeration but while sleepwalking numbers are metaphors and become fluid. For example you will probably already have noticed that your erections are larger and more painful. Be careful. If not assuaged they can lead to murder and suicide. The increase in size is due in part to lowered air resistance at higher altitudes, in part to increased energy streamings. The ancient Tibetans noticed this phenomenon and called it long duck. It is said that an oriental princess kept a pleasure palace in the Himalayas where she would excite her male slaves to the point of long duck and then have their organs severed and cooked. A version of this dish was brought back to middle Europe by the Mongols as sausage and is thought to be the origin of our own hot dog. Also ten-geek is a time. It's the name you give to the era as you now sense it, like twentieth century. For example this year would be ten-geek seven six. It's the kind of change in the time sense that happens after some kind of upheave, when everything turns over, when the words explode on the page, and you get 14th Brumaire or whatever. This means a major refocussing. Maybe what was worth it before isn't worth it now. A child dies or maybe something just clicks in your head one day. Suddenly the sphere of action seems pointless. Sex is no longer of great interest. Power is seedy. Money is boring. Friendship isn't serious, or isn't enough. Love is an exile's nostalgia. What remains is a kind of, let's say, painting. But painting of what? What is it that we sleepwalkers, in our trance, try to do? Let's try not to be frivolous about the thing, let's try not to evade the intelligence of it. What is that pure thing? Once a long time ago Juanitito and I were lovers, you didn't know that. He was what they call a great lover, I hesitate to use the cliche, even out here in the Rocky Mountains, but he was a great lover, believe me it was thrilling.

He came to me every day at dawn.

One morning he came and I knew he'd been with another woman that night.

This happened sometimes and I didn't care. He

was a buck and I didn't care as long as he kept bucking.

Afterward he went to work, he worked in a hospital. As an orderly.

The woman was a nurse he started going out with after work.

They would go listen to a group called the Ten Geek Jazz Band.

The band was named for its leader, Jan ten Geek.

A dutchman who came to this country after WWII.

He was in the resistance as an adolescent, was caught by the Nazis in 1943, sent to a concentration camp.

He lived.

Learned to play horn in the Black ghetto in Detroit.

He had lost his voice in the camp. Shock.

That was the cool jazz era, he was sort of like a mute Chet Baker. Not great but sometimes he could really go crazy.

I mean he was really saying something, mostly to himself but not bad for Denver: fuck you, screw my pussy, eat my shit and I'll suck your tit.

That kind of thing. Wang wang wang wang. I mean what's this allabout.

Well at that time Juanitito was known as a great stud, that's why they called him Dong Wang.

Well the nurse was named Marge, a blond, and that night Jan was just going crazy up there, too much, she got totally turned on.

Sonofabitch. Gogogogo.

Anyways she goes back to say hello at the break.

And Dong catches them outside the club in the back alley and she was doing something terrible and awful and obscene to him I won't even mention what it was.

She was sucking his cock.

Oh my god. The blower blowed.

Jan had a hard case of long duck, it was very embareassing.

To make a long story short the three of them became good friends. There are little third rate scenes like this going on all over America. You might say it's the essential flavor of the country.

It's so *good*.

I mean people just sort of break *loose*.

And then it turns out there's nothing to break loose *to*.

And that's *it*.

So Dong Wang ends up driving a delivery truck in Rapid City. So what?

It's the tip of that long line we keep drawing, each one of us.

It's part of the big picture we're all painting together.

The big picture is that there is no big picture. That's why we keep painting it.

The result is often "withdrawal of physical support, leading to separation anxiety."

The result is often limbo of used band-aids.

The result is unexpected.

It is not even a result.

immersion in space
grey song of metro
swarm of possibiliti
es terminals   geomet
ry of helical acid o
f angelic degradations
autohypnosis of soli
tude   thrust of want
raw information bodi
es don't lie   voyeur
of self   freeways of

mind   prosody of eve
nt conjunctions of c
hance minimize rolle
rcoasters   of   privacy
do interiors exist a
bscess of soul the lo
ose ends of a petty
denouement   sonic s
nob angelic wipeout s
ongs translate nothi
ng into something   s
pontaneous nomad   f
reeway of mind

5   Too much information leads elsewhere. Time pisses away oh
         yes. Immersion in space is best. Because there is no subject.
&   It's not about what's happening. Terminals initiate agenda of
         chance. Or geometry of helical acid. Grey song of the metro.
10   A coffee in the cafe. Happening is what it's about.

         Smudge of ancient city in rain constantly erased and rewrit-
         ten. Swarm of possibilities whiz he's one hey let's go man.
         Grey streets headline I. P. Daly In Paris quick steps. Then
         lost in markets no understand what talk is noise. Quick steps
         bump no understand before long very pleasant who. Swarm
         of street mysterious glances missed chances toward meeting
         where. You want hour love give money you what is every-
         thing. I. P. Daly am I do I no understand walk. Possibly you
         explain me if I meet you here when. If it's you who am I why
         do I do.

         I know what you want she said you want what you know you
         think I. You are gifted with a total absence of taste he told
         her you want to. Come and go I like it that way she said

terminals where you begin and. You understand what's happening it's complicated and puerile right an affair of voluptuous humiliations he. It's simple we talk because there's nothing to say but we need to say it. He come off it emotions don't count that is to say geometry of helical acid. She because ideas because premeditation because future you are a voyeur of yourself imposition of. You get off on angelic degradations but that gets us nowhere try conjunctions of chance. I don't have to get anywhere I'm here she said admittedly that has its pathos. He the immersion of discrimination in space the French view of Grand Canyon too big.

He had to go out and get some things because there was nothing in the apartment so after breakfast he. First he went to one store but he was told it was the wrong one but they told him that. He bought some of these and none of those but later he discovered they were the wrong ones anyway so. The market was going full swarm messages whizzing through the air messages he couldn't understand confections for tongue not ear. Then bought a newspaper and went for a coffee in the cafe the headline said I. P. Daly In Paris. Terribly in the first place was seriously considering amnesia couldn't get started because he couldn't remember about who or what. Said you are American they talked about it the only thing inevitable in New York is death and taxis she. Remember when I said you are my knife I am your fork I must have been lying intervention of distances. To the tobacco store for stamps to the druggery for tacks grey song of metro yesterday was a long time ago. A mess sperm spots on the blanket he must have been making love with someone or someone must have been.

Trippy autohypnosis of solitude what can I tell you sensual deprivation paranoia delusions of power bestial revery schizzy mood zoom ecstasy psychic power of lonely apartments. Getting off on terminal gratifications dishevelments of Fridays vocabulary of torpid interiors of bodies deranged plunge into amnesiac organs thrust of want throb of lack. Then beyond irony the curtain rises for the first time little by little thrust from the cunt wingtips first white but covered with blood it. Before long released power sound not articulation a song a song a chant oh yes time pisses away immersion in space is best that is. That is to say that is to say high looped it goes around around he takes everything he can get his hands on his way. She must have been lying she said because she wasn't her body because bodies don't lie blood and hair autopsychosis of raw information struggles against mother. Snatch rut guzzle snout torpor in the sun in sun pink butterfly flutters who are you torpid dormant viscous strange lacunae mute drenched with semen. I. P. Daly labeled phallocrat I. P. Daly cements relations with sperm I. P. Daly destroys brain cells through masturbation I. P. Daly solipsist who. The angel shakes out his bloody wings wings of autopsy and seduction suck dreams luxurious submissions sonic vacuums visual splendors infantile slurp of visceral slop. Remember he can't remember he can't remember he can't remember he doesn't want to he can't remember he can't remember he can't remember he can't.

Everything was so small he kept knocking it over and breaking it meantime back there the search for the great white fish continues and somewhere an enormous wave is breaking. The day he met her in the cafe got such a hit off her energy was insomniac all night ran along the Seine at dawn thinking jesus christ these Americaines. Total absence of taste leading to nostalgia for the mud the mud of the Colorado sucking out Grand Canyon watering melons of Southern California electrifying the network of Los Angeles. Back there they talk not to mean they talk to say was on the point of forgetting who he was in his head though still chasing the great white fish. Intervention of distances voyeur of self esthetic of molecular compositions moving through grid of chance immersion in space terminal gratifications she opened her mouth to speak a pink butterfly flew. Stupendous prosody of event alone anneals abscess of soul thus the freeways of the mind are laid bare to the hooves of oxen she murmured let's get going everything is. Each night before going to bed they talked about the big bang everything is widening opening out how much further is it for example from Biloxi to the Sandwich Islands. Keeps getting bigger lips tremble for time pisses communication lost amid white song of galaxy whizzing through star swarm white fish sperm blob amnesiac cosmos sucking power of absence mother. It happened that caught between nostalgia of past and pathos of present necessity of future propagated duplicity of act you're the greatest show on earth sweet heart voyeur of self. Suppose one could eat the great white fish suppose one did suppose suppose an enormous wave breaking suppose it's breaking in you suppose tremendous events tremble on your tip bang.

Someone has been using his toothbrush in his apartment his things aren't in the same place or maybe they never were a window open where a window was closed dishes dirty that were clean who. He was beginning to dope out the situation it was like submerged in her experience like she couldn't be aware of anything besides what she was doing and he was starting to do it too. It was admirable when it was admirable this flowing through life as if a river totally responsive to the prosody of event you are what you do red white and blue carefree thoughtless ruthless it. He into something heavy she feeling light he groping for poetry of pure consciousness she acting out infolding of his meditation exfoliation of her desire he sucks her in she sucks him out around around. Getting off on dishevelments of Fridays was not enough angular dishabillements angelic degradations voluptuous submissions time pisses away oh yes on other hand conjunctions of chance psychosis of too much information pathology of not enough. Of course but supposing the roofs were on the trees lacking a technology of rotation then who needs a program for interiors helical coils but California is not the world full of mysterious changes no. Okay time to stop jerking off splendid animals crave expansive continuities talking thinking loving eating walking seeing planning hearing yearning I. P. Daly In Paris haul ass out of the Louvre and into the rues. You can feel and feel but fact remains fact his letters to his lovers lacked conviction he could barely remember who they were was forgetting himself leaving himself behind then looped back anguish when she. Told the woman across the hall taste angel song power mother wings of autopsy and seduction white fish terminal prosody of event absence amnesia of cosmos bodies naked in time yearning space immersion meat angel. He went to the pharmacy he went to the bakery he went to the grocery he went to the laundry he went to the butcher he went to the cleaner everything was getting further apart.

And then street musicians on the Place soul rock blues Americans had a big crowd a hard black a brown with ear ring a slobby biker type they were tough old cowboy boots driving hard and they were making money. And then green cars zipping through blue streets red cars zipping through brown streets yellow cars zipping through black streets red fires white fires whizzing everything zigging through everything itself zagging and then buzzing and then swarming and then and. And then and then the repulsive old lady the girl who kept looking the stoned American staccato blacks sinuous yellows pearly greys grey blue blue grey hey guy down there pardon what language you speak no money for bread the. And then broken glass covers the Place like snow the left the right who knows what he said corpses floating down the river two empty shoes on the quai where a moment before tends to minimize roller coasters of privacy. And then the bitter honeymoon becomes the trivia of the enormity of the interiors of the afternoons of the Fridays of the woman across eerie halls as you read in the paper the next day I. P. Daly In Paris. And then the great white fish comes home the power the venom the anger the contempt the fear the dishevelments of Fridays are not enough the vain the vacuum the black suck of nothing dazzling who knocked up the void. And then we broke out blazing on motorcycles of Beethoven but that dies too in the exhaust fumes of the mind ending in beggars and loonies so we ate pie and continued she embedded in seven nostalgias of the future. And then he started venting venting spew did it in the street not in the dark corners neither where it saith thou shalt not right there in the middle and he did it every day and was the big cuchifrito. And then experimenting with insertions they wondered what was left after the demystification of desire differentiation being possibly still possible via helical acid terminals of chance do interiors exist after all the great white fish with its black heart or. And then stupor misery waiting for and then and then walking and then waiting and then talking and then shopping and then eating and then sleeping and then nothing and then white rage proof because what waits for and then.

So bitter fabrications became a bridge and icy castles glinting steely blue we are the loose ends of a petty denouement she said and went to a movie he fungoed line drives against the back fence thinking jagged bottles maybe and praying for vast distances. Speedometers set too fast give illusions that one is getting there faster than one is which is in fact the way all American speedometers are set but the angel goes nowhere faster than the speed of light which is the same as sitting still yes. You have to be hard to keep your mind on it in a straight line old cowboy boots help he said and slugged another one over second base in his head surrounded by crap the worst being your own I mean why not just die. She asked after spending ten years trying dissolve your character finally succeeding or become blue crystals none of it makes much difference possibly entertain thoughts of original stigmata to swing with black heart of white fish though we know it doesn't work even in song. And so in anterooms of tomorrow we exteriorize one hard white line defining black cowboy angel drive keeps mind on making money via song bridge good bitter brittle glass of self shatters duplicity becoming multiplicity becoming becoming the the the the the the the. Skateboards of fate slightly out of control these innings happens ends of errands in cafes happens next to happens lost key and then all slightly oblique as always an opening baffles of inertia into interior overdrive helical plasma uncoils into air current events ensue how. Lymph sperm spit blood scumbag of night small groups of two or four murmuring oil discovered in flower pot and then the steamroller and then flat tire the beauty of event is ugly total lack of taste Coney Island whitefish exploding unguided missile of time. All information leads here constantly erased and rewritten but what about what about meanwhile tomorrow doesn't exist or yesterday on the high wire conjunctions of chance in States life consists of driving straight ahead now it's all back and forth he said take a walk. He thought about thinking all week all week he thought about thinking nothing was happening then he thought about harpoons but it was still about about about back and forth back and forth he knew the alarm was about to ring hauled ass into rues. It was raining out he stopped in a cafe then he walked along the river then he had to meet somebody who wasn't there so he went to a movie then he called a lover then he made love then he left then he stopped.

In a cafe where dead ends stop here absolutely terminal dynaflow angel steps through shattered glass with just enough information to decode the cries of the rues of the

nights of the dreams of amnesiac maternal erasures angelic
wipeout songs dictate another version sitting in rooms translating nothing into something. Or collaborating in always
fatal prosody of event wondering whether one can toboggan
nowhere fast enough hand shaking bought a lottery ticket
each day never looking to see if he won took another airplane
baggage lost found takes care of itself deep in heart of power
fish find freedom there. Once hope relinquished in river
empty shoes racing for last metro late night lost walking
pleasure harpoon street lights lance abscess of soul terrorist
headlines claim I. P. Daly In Paris whizzing in crazy horse
taxi cabs zig of inside through zag of out through sense
unique sense always unique. Though what the hell if bad
oysters greet the weary traveler in mid carouse he still
moves ahead nor do we say the repetitions of love are all
the same and therefore fuck it I'm going out for a
McDonaldburger still he could spontaneous nomad prowls
boulevards not thinking happening. Knowing event is language too measured by solar arithmetic though immersion
in space best the couples holding hands thinks former wise
guy children dreaming cat sleep of apartments clock tick
peace floating above street shouts white static cosmos meat
angel singing silent self speeding still hydrogen hiss vast
openings closings. Maternal terminals of black radiance pull
backwards energize drive toward confrontations of helical
acid and conjunctions of chance in any cafe conditional ran-
dom bistros start happening a language a language we don't
understand white noise of event what is everything you explain me who am I why do I do. You are the cante jondo of
angelic speech a song decoded only in event in early morning walks to fetch croissants missed taxis after last metro
chance rendez vous with Brooklyn letters lost in mail which
decoded is another code angelic still frightening improbable
how much information leads here while. Fear of necessary
losses the girl was so frightened she turned blonde and
etherealized now she flaps around the ceilings of old
churches shedding feathers and digging Monteverdi others

read Nietzsche don't put it down nor fishing in ferocious surf nor doodles arising where ho meets hum these beautiful abstractions. Though are not for you permanent resident of nowhere city forager of five and ten voyager of vapid adventures sonic snob now feed the cat now bomb the delicatessen now eat the breakfast now make the love now picket the zeitgeist with confused manifestations now rev ferocious motorcycles of lettuce. Which nevertheless hack hard white line cashing blue crystals making money feed white fish for darkness straight ahead doing business with stars in correspondences of metros petit bourgeois your trip traces trivial continuities among grandiose disruptions sucks venom finds oil wells in flower pots politicizes ganglia make something of it.

another country inte
rsect   same place sa
me time blue nail po
lish stupid people l
augh   same box fath
er's organ still insid
e her   another music
music of dna doublin
g experience charti
ng flow   things he r
emembers   another c
ountry

B   X arrives at the airport and t
O   akes a cab to C-5 he calls K f
X   or directions then walks to a
E   location in east C-5 where he
S   meets U in her apartment X ide
ntifies himself by reference t
o a contact named R who is in
another country X spends fifte
en minutes indicating essentia

ls U spends fifteen minutes indicating essentials the two se
gments of fifteen minutes are
not consecutive but interspers
ed X using some minutes th
en U using some minutes and so
on in other words they had a c
onversation after thirty minut
es each knows where the other
is at partly what it amounts t
o is they are both in C-5 it is ten oclock in the evening X
is bored and exasperated he kn
ows no one here and he doesn't
speak the language the people
at K have placed him in a bad
hotel U is interested in his s
ituation partly because of the
contact with R X is suffering
considerable fatigue as he has
been travelling strenuously for some days despite this becau
se he is bored and exasperated
because he is staying in a bad
hotel and because he is intere
sted in U and her situation an
d the possibilities of that si
tuation he asks her to go with
him to the famous Uncle P in A
-4 just across the line from A
-5 and she agrees they take a cab to A-4 in Uncle P they sit
at the bar and listen to the s
inger X starts drinking long b
eer each beer takes seven minu
tes to draw they take longer t
o draw than they take to drink
after a while M comes over M i
s a disk jockey and she is cov
ering the club for some magazi

ne M says she is about to get fired for sexist reasons she s
ays she has a lot of lovers sh
e says there is a lot of grass
around she says she doesn't ha
ve time for long relationships
with men or deep ones they int
erfere with her career she ord
ers a round of Southern Comfor
t X gulps his between two long
beers M says she hates her father M says she was in New York
with her boyfriend M does not
think the woman who is singing
is a very good singer she says
it's all a matter of who you i
ntersect with she says she bel
ieves in being kind to her fri
ends H and A come over to talk
H is dressed in a man's cap an
d jacket with spots of rouge on her cheeks A says she is not
drunk but tipsy she has been i
n a Greek place all evening dr
inking retsina and dancing she
is wearing silver glitter stoc
kings and her fingernails are
painted bright purple she says
she is going to Philadelphia a
nd is celebrating and that she
comes here every night after midnight when admission is free
and that she is a friend of Un
cle P at least until he wanted
to make love and she didn't sh
e says U is really extraordina
ry she says she wants to go to
a transvestite bar X is tired
and goes back to his bad hotel
in C-5 the last thing he notic

es is that A is dancing with H lunch with the Professordocto
r in the eastern sector of D-6
A turns up U turns up as well
as young W who seems to be the
boyfriend of U and possibly al
so of A along with some others
A has a dreamy hangover she
was up till four one of the othe
rs thinks X should go to Bali
and offers to take him tomorrow to I-10 which is way off the
map and very picturesque A has
to go to C-5 later about Phila
delphia C-5 is where U lives a
nd is also X's box young W als
o has to go to C-5 and happens
to have a car so he gives them
all a ride to C-5 where their
comings and goings happen to i
ntersect at a certain hour in U's apartment young W says he
doesn't feel the need for drug
s or alcohol he says he can ha
ve all the experiences they br
ing without them except says X
the experience of being drunk
or high A says having a new lo
ver is like having a baby quot
ing American poem young W
says he has travelled across the States by car U says she has
been in Oklahoma and met·Indi
ans A goes to see about Philade
lphia young W says his father
is a church organist he has to
go somewhere but it's in the s
ame box so they will all meet
after dinner and go to another
box that's more fun X asks if

young W doesn't feel bad about leaving them together U says
she and young W have decided
not to become lovers they had
a long talk they are always tog
ether because they always happ
en to be in the same place at t
he same time they are both fri
ends of the Professordoctor U
says she gets along well with
her mother but doesn't talk with her father X guesses that h
er father is about the same ag
e as the Professordoctor who h
appens to be in the same place
at the same time or maybe even
as he X X asks whose place she
went to late last night from U
ncle P if not young W's U says
she always goes to see the sam
e boy the same time the same place X notes that he and U are
in the same place at the same
time U asks him what he dream
ed last night she says people h
ere believe the first time you
dream in a new place the dream
comes true X says he dreamed t
hey made love U says she wants
to go to another box she says
they will not make love this time or next time either she th
inks that the dream is complet
ely out of place at the same t
ime they are holding hands and
fondling one another after a w
hile it turns out they really
are in the same place by the t
ime they make love and eat din
ner it is time to meet A and y

oung W in another place in the same box X wonders why since
he feels A doesn't like him U
says no they are meeting becau
se A said she wants to spend m
ore time with him they all go
in young W's car to a bar A kn
ows in X guesses D-3 where X s
its next to A who is wearing g
reen nail polish A says the ne
xt night she will go to a Greek place she knows with friends
and they will drink retsina an
d then they will go to a tran
svestite place she knows X say
s he will go too A says she li
kes to go out dressed in men's
clothes she says stupid people
laugh they drop U off at the s
ame place the same time the ne
xt morning U is supposed to come to X's place in C-5 but she
is late and there is no time t
hen X is supposed to come to U
's place in C-5 that afternoon
but he is late and there is no
time then A is supposed to com
e to X's place in the evening
to take him to the Greek place
but she brings some grass whic
h they smoke and forget about the time and then they are lat
e and A says her boyfriend is
waiting at the Greek place and
she tries to call him but can'
t so they walk from X's place
in C-5 all the way to the Gree
k place in D-4 and then A deci
des that instead of meeting he
r boyfriend at the Greek place

in D-4 she will go with X to an Italian place in E-3 where s
he knows the owner so she stop
s off at the Greek place and t
ells her boyfriend that she wa
nts to be alone with X and the
n they walk all the way to E-3
E-3 is completely occupied by
a famous sex district the nigh
t is very cold by the time the
y get to the Italian place they are very cold so they drink
a lot to warm up it happens to
be the owner's birthday so the
Italian place is very festive an
d very crowded but A knows th
e owner and the headwaiter wh
o wants to sleep with her and
the waiters so soon they have
a pleasant table and very good
food more good wine and they are nice and warm and X asks
if her boyfriend didn't feel b
ad and A says yes but she told
him to expect things like this
and he is there at the Greek p
lace anyway with his old girlf
riend who he wanted her to me
et and that the night they met
in Uncle P she went home with
H and her boyfriend and two of her friends and they all got u
ndressed and A and H fondled
one another while they watched
and encouraged the boys as they
played with one another like c
hildren sucking and masturbati
ng all very relaxed she says a
nd very liberating to do that
was why she had a dreamy hango

ver the next day because she kept thinking about it all day
A is wearing blue nail polish alternately light and dark on adjacent fingers A says she ha tes her father she says young W is not her lover but her good friend she says young W has ne ver made love she says he says he doesn't want to she says th ey often travel together and she tries to teach him things b ut it's very difficult she says young W is very much in love w ith U who has a boyfriend she loves A says she had a boyfrie nd who she really loved but sh e found out he was seriously c razy A says young W doesn't un derstand those things when she told him she was attracted to X he couldn't understand why s he told him she liked the way X talked the way he moved he s till couldn't understand she s ays having a new lover is like having a baby they walk down t o the harbor through the sex d istrict and listen to the fogh orns then they take a cab to A 's apartment in B-3 where'A gets a call from H in the Greek place who says her boyfriend i s very drunk and is she coming A says no and X and A make lov e and A tells him this is the first time she swallowed it an d then they go to sleep togeth er the next day after a rendez vous in B-5 he checks by U's p

lace in C-5 who happens to be there with young W who always
has a pronounced air of melanc
holy around U tone of love unr
equited almost quaint X won
ders about the energy required
to sustain his inhibitions alw
ays in the same place as these
attractive women but as if in
the wrong time X wonders if it
has something to do with his father's organ if there is a mu
sic that transcends the organi
sm beyond its time and place t
hat young W can still hear whi
le X and U and A are left with
proximity and gratification an
d if there is if it's the musi
c young W hears or it that's th
e music of doom or if there's an
other music A and U are beginning to dance to as they hop fro
m box to box U says there is a k
ind of classical music for eve
ry time of day but doesn't und
erstand jazz while A prefers j
azz and rock and bouzooki musi
c X asks U how they get along
U says they are very different
but they are beginning to unde
rstand one another X takes U to his place because they need
to be alone where they make lo
ve U says she wants X to under
stand that she really likes th
e way he makes love to her she
says it's hard for her to make
love with her boyfriend afterw
ards when X is literally still
inside her but she says her bo

yfriend gets very excited making love to her after she has m
ade love to someone else even
though he doesn't know she has
X wonders what music her boyf
riend hears then the music of r
ut he says the music of genes
the music of DNA is dynamite U
asks X if he really dreamed th
ey made love X says no but he
really wanted to music of genes really wanted music of gene
ration or dissipation dance of
life or death or both they tak
e the S line to a box off the
map to eat in a Greek restauran
t full of tough young English
sailors after which X is suppo
sed to meet A and U is suppose
d to meet her boyfriend X tel
ls U he slept with A U says she thought that was going to ha
ppen U says she first got inte
rested in America through the
musical Oklahoma then went
to Oklahoma to visit a boyfrie
nd she met in England U says s
he's told her parents about X
she says they warned her not to
wait till she got married she
says she's been with her boyfriend since she was a teenager
X calls A she asks if he told
U he says yes she says that's
good the game continues A's m
ove she says she wants to meet
them both in another box they
all meet in another Greek plac
e in X guesses around C-3 A sa
ys she is surprised U made lov

e with X X says A misunderstands U's nature her ability to p
lunge though she seems conserv
ative he says U is more like h
er than A thinks U says she wi
shes she could go home with bo
th of them X says she can A sa
ys she should U says she can't
she has to meet her boyfriend
A says she spent the evening w
ith her boyfriend and just left him U and A are holding hand
s in X's lap then they begin f
ondling one another X is petti
ng both then gets embarrassed
particularly because of one wo
man across the room staring at
them and grinning he has the f
eeling they are creating a pub
lic scandal that they will be
thrown out at least and possibly arrested then the woman acr
oss the room comes over smilin
g and says I'm not laughing at
you I'm laughing with you then
U calls her boyfriend and tells
him she's going to A's when th
ey get up to leave the owner c
omes over and says he wishes h
e could have spent more time w
ith them but his girlfriend was there and the woman across t
he room asks how are you going
to arrange it tonight X has th
e feeling she wants to come al
ong too and begins to feel the
need for some sort of traffic
control some kind of flow cha
rt for his experience always d
oubled as it is by reflection
experience and reflection unif

ied in charting flow through f
lats and sharps of feeling the
y take a cab to A's place in B
-3 where A makes some hash tea
and X opens a bottle of retsin
a they brought from the Greek
place and kisses their faces a
nd necks XXXXXXXXXXXXX
XXXXXXXX jesus christ says
A there were three things he w
as to remember afterward one m
aking love to A two A's hand o
n his balls guiding him in and
out of U three after all that
feeling lonely and jealous as
A and U made love realizing th
at was checkmate the point of
the game all along but even so
finished they came back to kee

p him company one each side X wakes up between A and U fee
ling after three hours sleep l
ike he's slept for days feelin
g very friendly leaves them to
gether goes to hotel finds a m
essage from K saying this has
all been a mistake he's not su
pposed to be in this city goes
to airport takes plane to anot
her city AU AU AU AU AU

claude balls wun hu
ng lo   i. bitchakoko
ff   bwana suk   conju
ring power of fictio
n   floating down the
river on a marble sl

ab   olaf eats meat l
oaf   one ton soup   g
et the pigture you f
rig some ducks   eye
music   word bombs

T   This is the part of THE ENDLESS SHORT STORY about going to
H   San Francisco and Andreie Codrescu asking me for a story
I   for a magazine and some other things I don't know what they
S   are yet and the rules for it are write fast because he needs it
     right away totla improvisation and also and most important
I   don't correct typing. The reason this is so important is that
S   it's such a relief all my life I've been in bondage to this
     machine I have no aptitude for and now — total freedom — at
T   last. $9#*¢=×/U! Momentous. Other variables are that
H   while I'm doing this story I have to decide whether to accept
E   a job at the Iowa Writer's Workshop for the coming
     smester — they have smesters out there in California we use
P   the qwater system. Also the story about Harry the Dick and
A   Wun Hung Lo in Chinatown this is how that came about.
R   One morning i was awakened by a phone
T   from SF it was Calude Balls I recognize
         him right away from his accent. He says
         he has an iteresting idea about the deat
         of language — these Frenchman with their
         absrtactions he says what people are rea
         interested in now adays is looking at pi
         so what we do is instead of language we
         give them word pictures well this strike
         me as a pretty harebrained idea but it s
         happens that it fits in with my plot to
         destroy the Egnlish language and so I ag
         to come up there to talk with him about
         it and to provide cover I arrange to giv
         a reading from my writing at Hayward Sta
         But to get back to Claude Balls his idea

is for example you make up word bombs fo
example you take the phrase wordbombs
roll it up into a ball:

```
        w
       ord            wo
       bomb           rdbo
        s             mb
                       s
```

```
w
 o     o
  o  m   s  r
  b    b
  d
```

Then you throw them at somebody and
they explode into meaning.

But I have to think
about this Iowa busi
more. Just had anot
call interruption ab
another job this tim
the Writers in the Sc
program two jobs in
one day not bad I no
tice that whenever I
start thinking about
getting jobs in my w
I mean writing about
it I start getting j
like example it happ
at the end of UP & o
stories too I mean l
the phone starts rin
notice how you don't
need the whole word
to understand what I
talking about and yo

want to know why I w
to destroy the Engli
language eleiminate
waste that's why a l
of reasons I can't e
think of them all ri
now. Anyway back to
how when I write abo
jobs I get them (kno
wood) it's part of w
I call the conjuring
power of fiction in
which I include poet
A very curious busin
many times I've writ
things and then they
come true. It's got
to do with writing a
magic. See for exam
that part of the art
about the strange con
nec bwetween my boo
and Casteneda's. Onlx
trouble is that you
can't use it on purp
for example if I were
to now write about h
I'm going to make a
million bucks it wou
work I feel. He who
looks doesn't find.

But let's get back t
the story. When we
last saw Claude Ball
he was on the phone
with his hysterical
plan about wordbombs

actually that was my hysterical plan mon dieu this is getting me nowhere I have to call Iowa in just a few minutes I mena I'd like to go to Iowas but 3½ months in the snow away from Lynn of course there'd be lots of vestals to k me warm I've heqrd a thar place they use coeds for radiators just kidding woman's lib. Still do I wan th t kind oc thing n what about finishing my novel and then re how tedious Sarah La College got?

So there I was floati down the river on a marble slab when sud a green slimy arm re up out of the water it was Claude Balls "Feelthy peekture Mee he says. I pull him up beside me "Listen Claude," I say, "You' right. People don't want to read they wa to *have* read without going through the tr dig? like I just hea over the radio even

LIFE magazine is goi
out of business so w
you want from me? W
you expect I should
do about it or somet
? Besides what's in
it for me? Sure I k
the answer but I'm n
going to tell you.
"There are ways of m
people talk bwana Suk
Bwana Suk is one of
the pen names I use
in my stories, for Af
sections. To be per
rank I never did li
Claude Balls very mu
I felt he didn't rea
represent the true g
and genius of his peo
I rolled a word up a
threw it at him:

   h u
s m k
  c c

When it hit him he r
blew up face purple
hands clawing at his
throat he staggered
to the edge of the r
and fell back into th
water. And yet I wi
leave a clue.
This is the clu
The typewriter
is my instrumen
I sit before it

improvising on
the keyboard li
P. Quince and y
to her the musi
you must read t
score. Like pa
painting that is
writing is eye
music. Yoi yoi
    One might
    go even f
    further   a
       and
         P
         r
         o
         p
         o
         s
         e
But the technol
won't allow, th
margin mechanis
in   this   case.
And so we wave
goodbye to the
natives, and as
the sun sets it
occurs to me th
John Ashbry wo
do better to Wri
his prose in ve
thin   columns.
Very thin colum
And now a secre
message to Andr
Rumanian: Vash

z'nage' lftu' c
vspschze. No?
Well I just called Iox
to tell them I'm not
going but Iowa isn't
home. Soon I'll be
on my way to meet Unc
Uncle Dookis I have
to finish this befor
then. I think the t
typewriter is broke
or maybe it just don
wanna rite Uncle Doo
Uncle Dookis Uncle D
Dookis Sookis. See/
And I haven't even g
into the story about
Harry the Nark and W
Wun Hung Lo in China
It goes something like this.
Wun Hung Lo reaches into his p
for some bills to pay Harry's
"vig" and instead pulls out a
bill size note accidentally s
into Harry's reasy palm it s
"CLAUDE BALLS EXISTENTIALIST
PIG" sgined xI. Bitchakokoff.
Him again. Well it xo hap ens
that Balls is just the man Har
the Narc's looking for on a ch
of jumping bail without "wiping
his nose". I mean Harry the N
reallywants this guy bad "vig"
or no "vig". Dig? This is no
joke because Harry is 6 foot 7
weihgs forty stone and proud o
it. I mean fat. Fat and full

of hate. That's why from now
on he follows Wun everywhere h
goes. Even to poetry readings
even to poetry readings by G.
Malange. So you begin to get
the pigture. The pigture is
that this pigturd porker muscl
in on a peaceful poetfest with
his nasty body oozing violence
Yoi yoi. I can write anywhere on the pa
yoi zoi. I want. Yoi yoi. Now it so hap
that Wun Hung Lo own this festaurant yes
festaurant that's a good one thnkyou oyp
in Chinatown named Kokoff's where the po
like to gather ets not lice. It's a Rus
restaurant I mean festaurant one of the
few in Chinatown and it's ownd by guess
who you're right I. Bitchakokoff accordi
to the law that all Chinese festaurants
are onwed by Rusians. Bitchakokoff is
unwed and a little cracjed knowing as he
does that his favorite tune is "Onward
Christian Soldiers" a religious fanatic
to boot. Yes a little S&m too I'm afrai
but mostly S the m he saves for mealtime
Well he sit down at table with us "the bell about to ring now
it can be toll" he say. He spic no good. Too many country no
good btween ear. What hoopin den with fat sizlle in fire.
Turns out Balls used to play for Booklyn Dodgers back in
1942. Harry order potsticker. One ton soup. You frig same
ducks. One hand up one behind back. Very reasona "Tho an'
I would be half in love with nonsense" say Andrei. When
Harry take out pitfall with head of wife cut out waite vomit.
"Went right Through windshield". The conversation turns
to Madame de Sevigny. Olaf eats meat loaf. Zong Yoi yoi. Hi
Uncle Dookis! Madame LaZonga! Come back again.

once upon a time   en
ergetic   activity   fol
low it to bar   i cou
ld look it up   blown
away off track   use
everything we're bei
ng written down what
's the real story   y
ou have to sign herd
s of swans live monk
ey brains   we become
characters who are b
eing narrated   nobod
y will touch the wom
an you're with unles
s   you want to just
watch the real story

D   "It's off?"
U   "Life is off. Now it's on."
C   "So when do you find out if it's working?"
K   "Blow into that one."
           "Testing. Testing testing testing. That may be the
T   best part of the tape. Do you think I hurt your cat's feel-
A   ings?"
P   "What's he doing?"
E   "The way I threw him out?"
           "I mean what's he doing right now, you can tell if his
feelings are hurt."
           "He's sniffing my books."
           "Well if he pees on them you know you hurt his
feelings."
           "And here's the other cat. The other cat is walking
through the room sneezing like a locomotive. Anyway the
point of this is to have a duck tape because we're having a
duck dinner."

"And you were going to tell me a story."

"I was going to tell you a story. Okay. Once upon a time, there was this love story. I don't like this beginning, and also the cat's sneezing like mad."

"Want me to go put her to bed?"

"No, I think she likes it here."

"What if we fed her a piece of duck fat, she'd really love that."

"Yeah. Well we got a lot of spare duck fat here. Oh god the other cat immediately got wind of it although he's in another room, as soon as we did that, where he couldn't possibly see what was going on, he immediately got wind of something being eaten."

"I'm not sure I like this being a love story. What about a like story?"

"All right, ducky, a like story. But you have to remember this is my story so I can do what I like in it. You just happen to be in it. But I guess you have certain rights as a character. Since I let you loose."

"Where did you meet this woman?"

"By an interesting coincidence, I met her exactly where you're going tomorrow."

"In Charlottesville, Virginia? I don't believe it."

"Isn't that an odd coincidence? I didn't even think of it till just this minute. You're going there tomorrow and that's where you grew up and that's your home and you're going to visit your family. What she was doing there I have no idea, I still have no idea. Except that she had come down from Swarthmore, is that near Swarthmore somewhere?"

"I used to drive down all the time when I was going to Swarthmore."

"So that's another coincidence, and she came down from Swarthmore and there was this incredibly boring party after some literary affair. This duck is improving. I think I'm getting to the good part."

"Have some more wine."

"Where was I? Oh yeah, this boring party and I was

there being bored."

"How long ago was this, anyway?"

"Must have been around nineteen seventy-three. Or two."

"That's a long time ago."

"Or four."

"She might have even been a student at the time."

"I think she was. She was definitely a student at Swarthmore. And she was working on the underground newspaper."

"I was working on the underground newspaper. When I was a student there."

"You see. Coincidence. She's blond too, like you."

"I'm not really blond."

"Well she's not really blond. Maybe this is a story about coincidence."

"Really. Anything can happen in a story."

"Right. And maybe it's not a true story. Anyway she was having an affair with the faculty advisor of the underground newspaper."

"Wait a minute. I was having an affair with the faculty advisor of the underground newspaper. What was his name?"

"Cut it out. Enough already."

"Are you sure it was seventy-three? Because I left in seventy-two."

"I'm not sure what years she was there."

"I wonder if he was cheating on me. What did you say her name was?"

"I didn't. I'm leaving that out of the story."

"So anyway you immediately recognized that this girl was a good kid. From what you told me before the story."

"Well I'm not so sure she was good I mean she is what she is, a mixture of good and bad. But anyway all this is a side track. The point is I was sitting there being very bored because I hate literary conferences, I know you're going to one tomorrow in Charlottesville. This is an incredible series of coincidences."

"Do you think I'll meet an interesting undergraduate from Swarthmore?"

"I hope not."

"I'm going to be busy."

"Well I was busy. Anyway I was busy relaxing at that point. And I noticed a lot of activity over to my right, and what I noticed about this activity was that there was this well known poet, whose name I'm leaving out of the story, who was obviously putting the make on this person, who I hadn't much noticed before, and now I just noticed because it was some kind of energetic activity. And I was watching out of one eye so to speak, not very interested, when suddenly, when suddenly this girl got up to get a drink, by this time it was very late toward the end of the evening, and as far as I could see this poet was having no success. And she got up to get a drink at the bar, and I noticed she had this really wonderful, beautiful ass. So of course my reaction to that, because she was facing the bar and her ass was toward me, was to get up and to sort of follow it to the bar."

"You sound like Harpo Marx. I'm surprised you didn't reach out and grab it."

"Well what I did was I said, 'Hi, would you like to come up to my room.' "

"An interesting approach."

"Well, that's what I said. And she said, 'Okay.' "

"Did she know who you were?"

"I don't know. And so we went off together just like that."

"Did you expect her to say okay?"

"It's like when you're betting on horses or something, you follow your instincts, I had no expectations."

"That's quite interesting. I mean it was a nice kind of approach but I wouldn't have expected her to say yes, I would have expected her to laugh, or talk to you or, you know, slow it down a little."

"Well she's always very impulsive I think. I later

discovered. I mean you'll see, because we made love very nicely, at least it was nice for me, and we finished making love —this girl had not said a word, except 'okay', from when I met her at the bar to when she went to my room, made love, she still hadn't said anything. Amazing."

"I don't know, I think it's a kind of common female ploy. I've used it at least twice myself."

"Why would you not say anything?"

"Just to see what would happen."

"What usually happens?"

"Well the first time I ever tried it I got so anguished that I got very uneasy about it. It was with a Frenchman in Italy, and we talked and went out together and went drinking."

"I thought you said the point was not to talk."

"But I never said anything, I never said what my name was, or identified myself, or gave any information about myself. And I finally got very uncomfortable with the whole situation, I felt as if I didn't exist. The second time it was with . . ."

"Did you make love with him?"

"Eventually, yes."

"Not that night?"

"I can't remember. I might have. I could look it up. Anyway the second time it was with a Turkish ice skating champion . . ."

"The Turkish ice skating champion with the unbuttoned shirt?"

"Yeah."

"That is, yours?"

"Yeah. Who I never said anything to. And he talked to me and I didn't talk to him. And eventually he asked me for my phone number and I wrote it on a dollar bill. And then months later somebody called me and said, 'Hey Pamela I've got one of your dollar bills.' Anyway he sounded really nice so I agreed to have a cup of coffee with him and it turned out he was a Nobel prize physicist who had just gotten divorced and I ended up having a long affair with him. And then after about five months one day he simply disappeared and it turned out he was a Russian spy."

"How do you know?"

"I read about it in the papers. It seems his cover was about to blow so he took off to Moscow with loads of top secret information."

"And you had no idea all that time?"

"No, I was completely blown away. I mean I thought it was a little odd he spent so much time playing with his short wave radio. And also he talked Russian in his sleep."

"Is this a true story?"

"Absolutely."

"And the Turkish ice skater?"

"I never saw him again."

"I know that's not true. Anyway. You got me completely off track."

"I'm sorry."

"That's your job, you're supposed to get me completely off track."

"That's all right, this is your story."

"I can already tell this story is going to be too long."

"Why don't you just use the parts that are most interesting?"

"No, what I like to do is I like to use everything. Anyway. So she left. Right after we made love. And I said, 'Hey wait a minute,' she was at the door, and she said, 'What?' like I couldn't think of anything to say, so I said, 'Do you have a cigarette,' so she left me a cigarette and she left."

"You didn't ask her name or anything?"

"I didn't have a chance. So the next morning as I was leaving for the airport, I saw her walking along with several other people and she looked highly embarrassed."

"She expected never to see you again."

"Probably. Anyway that was the beginning of the story. The next part of the story takes place some years later, as they say in novels, at I think another literary party in New

York. It must have been about four years later. Maybe five. And at this party, I was slightly loaded, and suddenly somebody taps me on the shoulder and says, 'Remember me?' and it was her."

"Did you remember her?"

"I think so, yeah. Obviously I did. I was very surprised. And this girl was living in New York and I think working as an editor somewhere and looking very pretty."

"You hadn't noticed the other time?"

"She was pretty then too. Very young though. Should I say though? I mean a kid."

"I know you don't like em young."

"You know nobody knows that you're a girl, I mean woman. Nobody knows that because this is written down. I mean they can't see us. We're being written down now. We are written down in effect."

"Oh no, they know I'm a woman because I was talking about writing my name down on dollar bills for men and things."

"That's true."

"In fact I'm sitting here with my shirt off, can't they tell?"

"No that's what they can't tell. They would be very surprised. It's a topless duck dinner story. And anyway. What's the real story here."

"Okay so you met her and she was looking very pretty."

"And of course we got together again and made love together and I got to know her a little bit more. And then for the next five years, what year are we now?"

"Nineteen eighty-four."

"For the next four or five years anyway, whenever I would go to New York I would curl this girl up, call this girl up."

"You want some more wine?"

"Better not. Oh well thanks."

"She never had a boyfriend?"

"She always had a boyfriend but she would never tell me about it. She once told me she was going out with a famous journalist, that was the maximum information I ever got out of her."

"She didn't mind making a place for you in her private life?"

"Yeah I thought that was very curious."

"I think it's darling, really nice."

"I thought it was nice actually. I thought it was nice from both sides. First of all that I would call her up always, second of all that she would usually get to see me. But, she was a bit crazy. That is sometimes she would make an appointment and she wouldn't show up, and I'd be left waiting in a bar or something like that."

"Oh I wouldn't like that much. I wouldn't give it more than one try I think."

"Usually I wouldn't give it more than one try, but in this case I gave it several tries. And I think that's the curious thing, part of the interest of the story is for some reason I was still motivated to get in touch with her, after she did those dumb things. So what's my story?"

"What do you think was going on with you?"

"Well I must have been fond of her."

"It sounds like it. You're still fond of her, aren't you?"

"Well, it was becoming a kind of friendship, and I also came to realize that was her frightened way of being ambivalent about wanting to see me in the middle of her intense famous reporter relation or whatever, at totally unpredictable intervals, I mean she's frightened of me too, at least that's what she says. And also sometimes she wouldn't make love with me when she was supposed to."

"What does that mean, supposed to?"

"Well I mean when we're in erotic situations, and then I would sort of have to make her, that was the routine, see. I think she's basically a very frightened person."

"Maybe she likes to be frightened."

"Last time I saw her which was about a week ago in

New York, she told me the story of her youth which I'd never heard before, and I think is very interesting and which I'll tell you, or retell you, did I tell you this before?"

"She was having incest with her father or something?"

"No as far as I know she never had incest with her father, that's a different story."

"What story is that?"

"That's the story about a girl who when she became a writer started making up these stories and she didn't know where they came from, about prepubescent girls having incest with various family members, she was from the south naturally, like you, and they started scaring her but she kept writing them anyway and suddenly one day she realized they were about her. She had just completely blanked it out. She confronted her father with it too."

"What happened?"

"He started drinking and drank for five days straight and they found him in the gutter."

"Alive?"

"Physically anyway. If you can call that alive. How many women are walking around with that kind of time bomb? Which probably never goes off in most cases. Just ticks their lives away to a certain sinister rhythm."

"Yuk. Yeah well I get all the stories mixed up after a while."

"Yeah well. That's good. It's all one big story."

"The endless short story."

"Right. What was I going to tell you, what story?"

"You were going to tell me the story of her youth."

"Oh yeah, right. But first how about taking your shirt off?"

"Why?"

"It's very encouraging to a story teller when he sees the audience can't keep its shirt on."

"I'll take my shirt and my pants off too if you like."

"No, this is only a topless short story. If it were a

bottomless short story it might never get told. It might drive me right out of my own story into real life. So keep your shirt on. Or at least keep your pants on."

"So what's the story?"

"Yeah so she was one of the first girls to go to Yale."

"I thought she went to Swarthmore."

"She did, she transferred after she dropped out. And apparently as a freshman got mixed up with some junky freak in New Haven who inveigled her to go home with him because he wanted to turn her on, first it was cocaine I guess, but she quickly became a junky. Imagine going to Yale at eighteen as a coed freshman being a secret junky. And she broke up with this guy apparently quite soon and then started hanging out in the New Haven Black section with this old Black junky who was her connection I guess, who would be turning her on all the time, and who would be getting her to do mildly adventurous things, like being a sexual decoy for robberies and stuff like that."

"What did she do, seduce the night watchman?"

"How did you know? More or less, without actually being seduced."

"That's right, you said she never gets hurt."

"Yeah, she's lucky."

"I'll bet it's not lucky, I'll bet it has something to do with the kind of vibes she puts out."

"Yeah imagine her going up to Harlem alone in the middle of the night for cocaine. Or being held tied up at gunpoint for three days because some dealers think she's a cop. Or making love on the floor in the middle of a shootout with the police. Or being chased by a pack of wild dogs in the Maine woods. Or adrift in a storm in the Carribean with a bunch of dope smugglers who don't know anything about boats. Or being kidnapped as a sacrificial victim on a jungle island. Or being tied to the railroad tracks with the train coming. Or being lured into an orgy club when high by some guy who picks her up in the street and then deserts her so they won't let her out."

"What was the end of that story, how did she finally get out?"

"I don't know she tried to run out the door without any clothes on and they dragged her back. I think they finally let her out by virtue of longevity."

"She stood at the door like dogs waiting to be let out."

"Or cats, right. Anyway, she reformed. And then she went to Swarthmore."

"That's where you go when you reform."

"I mean she didn't completely reform, she's very impulsive so she would do things like I would call her up in the middle of the night and she would come to my room at the Algonquin, in the middle of this story I was always staying at the Algonquin. I know it's the wrong crowd. And sometimes she would say she was going to come and would never show up. Sometimes she would show up with cocaine, she introduced me to cocaine for the first time."

"Did you like it?"

"Yeah I did, it was nice to make love with."

"I never made love with it I just used it for working. It's so expensive you have to use it for something productive, right."

"Well it's so chic you know. If you want to be like a hip L.A. used car salesman snort some coke. You realize we're being taped."

"Yeah but they don't know who I am, I'm safe. You have to sign the damn thing."

"Well that's why it's my story."

"I might put it on my curriculum vitae anyway."

"The end of the story, by the way, which I'll tell immediately, way before the end, is that she said why don't you write a story for the magazine I'm working for. So I said I'll write it about you, because I'm so chivalric. But of course they won't publish it because it's too real. This is not a tape, this is real life."

"Did you sleep with her that time in New York?"

"No. I would have except for the following incident

which I'm about to tell you. We met in a bar and I of course since she never wears any underwear and that always turns me on started caressing her in the bar you know sort of between buttons, and we were both getting sort of turned on and suddenly she looks up at me and says, 'I'm pregnant.' So I got you know, a little bit put off, and she got a little bit put off. Anyway, she wouldn't come back with me."

"Did she have the baby?"

"No. Next time I met her she seemed sad and looked very different. Grown up a little maybe. I don't think I'll send this to the magazine where she's working."

"I don't think that magazine would publish this story anyway."

"You don't?"

"I think they only publish stories that start she was tall and willowy and red headed and she turned off the water at the sink and dried her hands on the dish towel because the door bell was ringing. Isn't that the way those stories always start?"

"She says they never turn down anything good."

"And I used to think I was a duck but now I think I'm a swan."

"Have you ever been to Bruges? With all the swans?"

"That's where I'd like to go. Would you like to go to Bruges?"

"I'm tired of Bruges. And also, I didn't like the swans, I mean the swans there were so numerous, there were herds of swans, and they were very ferocious. You know swans are very big and strong, and they can be very mean, and they, you know, they can, I mean how do you feel when you start getting chased by a herd of fifty swans."

"There's some collective noun for swans."

"Swims. Swims of swans."

"Were you attacked by swans?"

"I was threatened by swans."

"I'll tell you one thing though, you hardly ever get a roast swan for dinner."

"I wonder what that would taste like. I wonder why you don't actually. I bet in China you get a roast swan, after all they make things like camel hump and elephant trunk."

"And live monkey and fried dog."

"Live monkey?"

"Don't you remember the monkey brain story? I think it's a big delicacy where you cut the top of the head off a living monkey and eat the brains out of the skull."

"Oh my god."

"Somebody ate it while they were in China."

"It makes me feel the top of my head. To make sure it's still there."

"You sure you weren't born in the year of the monkey?"

"They still actually do that? Under the enlightened communist regime."

"You *were* born in the year of the monkey."

"I was?"

"Somebody told me this monkey brain story I forget who it was. It was Y."

"Was he putting you on?"

"No. He was just eating monkey brains."

"Should I put him in the story? Or will he sue me?"

"Do you want to? It's your story."

"Well I don't know he just cropped up, I'm just worried about being sued. After all he's a famous lawyer."

"Well we didn't say anything about him why don't we drop it."

"I have to leave him out of the story?"

"Well I don't think you can be sued for anything so far. I mean I don't even remember if he ate the monkey brains."

"I wouldn't. I don't see how you can go out with somebody like that. Live monkey brains? Disgusting."

"There are a few things I have trouble eating. Sheep's eyes."

"Live monkey brains seems to be like being not only

a cannibal but a sadistic cannibal."

"I think the monkey dies when they cut its head open."

"Well I assume. Sooner or later."

"You're forgetting your story."

"So what. The real story is between us anyway. Did I get to the climax yet?"

"Well you haven't told the story yet. You haven't told anything about the sado-masochistic stuff."

"Oh the sado-masochistic stuff, I forgot about that. Can I put this in the story?"

"Sure. My name's not in there. Nobody will know who we are but Y."

"Y would know? Why would he know?"

"He's the only one who knows I go out with you and him. Besides you."

"You think you'll marry that guy?"

"I don't know he hasn't asked me."

"Well. I guess we never know what the future will bring."

"I certainly don't know. It's your story."

"Right. In fact don't you think it's time to make it clear to everybody that this is a story I'm making up and not a tape recording?"

"How do we do that?"

"Easy. Just add 'he said, she said' to everything we say. Then we become characters who are being narrated."

" 'Okay.' She said.

'See, it's not hard at all.' He said.

'No.'

She said.

'She said,' she mimicked.

'Anyway we were in a cab going to this sado-masochistic place because I'd said I'd heard of it when we couldn't get to see the movie we were going to see because it had changed, *Night Porter*.' He said. 'And I said,' he said, 'well, I know a, somebody, because I was just talking to this pornographic movie star, I mean star of pornographic movies, who told me about all these pornographic sado-masochistic places I'd never heard of before. And I said,' he said, 'I just happen to have in my pocket the address of some place that sounds like the plot of *Night Porter*,' he said.

'What's it called,' she said. She asked.

'What's it called,' he repeated. ' "The Inferno." No. "Hellzapoppin?" No,' he mused. 'Then she got into this fight with the cab driver on the way over there. And it was one of those fights that's like baiting people sexually,' he went on.

'Was the cab driver somebody attractive to her, do you think?' she asked.

'I don't think it mattered, I think what mattered was he was male and baitable. I think that's just her way of getting excited,' he speculated. 'I think finally she's turned on by this sadomaso scene because I said, going to this place, where apparently the scene is, as that pornographic movie star woman told me, nobody will touch the woman you're with unless you give them permission. And I said to my friend well that being the case do you want to just watch or do you want to participate and she said, *Participate*,' he said thoughtfully, crushing out his cigarette.' "

"I didn't know you smoked."

"Well I stopped, but I still like it, and in stories I can smoke without it being harmful to my health."

"In that case, can I have one?"

"Sure. In the story."

" 'What happened next,' she asked. Taking a deep drag on her cigarette.

'You smoke too much, ducky,' he snapped. 'Anyway,' he continued, 'we couldn't find the place and she kept baiting the cabbie, and finally he slams on the brakes and says, *Okay, you get off right here,*' he said. 'So I say, *Look if we get off here I'm not going to pay you,* because you know we're way over near the piers somewhere, really no man's land. And the guy gets out of the cab, opens the back door on her side and says, *Right well if you ain't paying me she's paying me,* and he starts pulling her out of the cab. Incredible. So naturally I run around to the other side of the cab and the guy pulls a gun on me,' he said.

'Wait a minute,' she said. 'This is the sado-masochistic part?'

'Yeah, I mean the scene she was getting into with the cabbie and we were on our way to an SM club.'

'I feel kind of confused about what was going on,' she objected.

'If you're confused, imagine the reader. You at least know me and can ask questions, the reader doesn't know me from a hole in the wall. And perhaps would rather know a hole in the wall. After all this sordid stuff about eating monkey brains. Famous lawyer eats live monkey brains. Sue me.'

'You forgot to say he said,' she said.

'He said,' he said.

'So what did you do with the cabbie?' she asked.

'I paid him, what do you think I do when people point guns at me. Meanwhile I can't tell whether she's terrified or getting off. Or both,' he speculated.

'Last time you told me this story you said you knocked him out with a karate chop,' she said.

'I did? Well maybe I knocked him out. Or maybe that was the other guy,' he wondered.

'Now come on, Norman. I want the real story. Did you go home with this girl?' she asked. 'What other guy?' she added.

'How come you're using my real name all of a sudden? You want everybody to know my real name?' he asked.

'Yes, I want you to use your real name because I want you to tell the real story,' she said.

'What do you call the real story?' he asked.

'I want to know whether you got into bed with this girl,' she said.

'I don't know whether I want to tell that part of the

story,' he answered.

'I don't know if I like this story,' she mused. 'It's too troubled.'

'That's all right, stories need conflict. Okay, I'll tell the real story but you have to promise not to interrupt,' he offered.

'Okay Norman,' she agreed.

'The real story was that they're in this crowded restaurant talking about going to this Hellzapoppin place or whatever it's called and he's trying to describe what this porn star told him it's supposed to be like. And there are these two guys at the next table who are eavesdropping and after a while they start snickering. So then he starts inventing obnoxious stories about how she likes to make love with dogs, isn't there a name for that?' he asked.

'Cocker sucker?' she ventured.

'Yeah maybe, so then they start making remarks and he tells them, *Shut up*, and they have, what do you call it, words. So then they're waiting for them outside. And then that's when he knocks the other guy out with a karate chop,' he said.

'Oh you didn't,' she objected.

'And anyway he manages to get her into a cab and takes her home. And she's really turned on by the fight, from which he has a bloody nose,' he went on.

'That's not true,' she interrupted.

'And she practically makes love to him in the cab,' he added.

'Come on, Norman,' she objected.

'But when they get into bed together she decides she doesn't want to make love, and by the time he convinces her to, he gets completely turned off,' he continued.

'You want to make love now?' she asked.

'Now? In the middle of the story?' he asked.

'We could use dots. You know, like he carried her into the bedroom dot dot dot dot. Two hours later he was in a cab to the airport,' she said.

'Right. Two hours. Two hours? I guess two hours,' he mused. 'Anyway when she realizes he's not going to make love to her this amazing thing happens. She's like leaning over him right. And he feels this single, huge tear splash on his chest. Just one tear, that's all, it must be about an inch across.'

'Are you sure she never gets hurt?' she asked.

'Not so sure, no,' he murmured.

'Anyway I don't believe it. I never cry one tear. When I cry I really cry. Lots of huge tears,' she said.

'And then he says, wiping his chest, *You know I don't really understand what's happening.*

And she says, *Neither do I.*

And he says, *That story you wanted me to write? I think I'm going to write the strange story of our history together, that way maybe we can figure out where we're at.*

And she says, *What if we discover we like one another more than we want to?*

And he says, *Too bad, ducky. The point is to try to be objective. Third person.*

And she says, *What does that mean, that I'm not going to be me in it?*

And he says, *That's right. And I'm not Norman Miller.*

And she says, *Why don't you use a tape recorder, so you can get at the real truth?*

And he says, *Recorders don't get at the truth, they only get at the facts, the only way you can get at the truth is to make it up. But I could make up using a tape recorder, that's not a bad idea.*

And she says, *And where will all this get us?*

And he says, *It will get us right here. Which is exactly where we're at.*

And she says, *What happens next?*

And he says, *Let me tell you a story. Not long ago I decided to tape a dinner conversation. I got these two volunteers, they were lovers, had a friend of mine cook them a*

*duck and bought them a lot of good wine. Well at first it was
pretty dull and I thought it was going to bomb, but then they
started getting loaded on the wine and the guy told the following story.*

— My problem, *he said,* is I don't have any sexual
fantasies. I guess I just lack imagination. So my thing is I sort
of hitch hike on other people's fantasies. As a result I often
find myself going out with some strange people. To wit,
Pamela over here.

— Are you going to start making up stories about me
again, *she said.*

— I don't make up stories, *he said,* I'm a lawyer. I deal
in facts. The fact is that Pamela here has nothing but fantasies. If you took away her fantasies she'd evaporate like a
ghost at dawn.

— Don't listen to him, *said Pamela.*

— That's why she's so sexy in those porn movies. She
really gets off on them.

— I was never in a porn movie.

— And if it's not exhibitionism it's masochism.

— You're just projecting your fantasy life onto me. As
usual.

— On top of that she's got a habit. That's how I met
her. I was defending her on a possession charge. She didn't
have enough money for my fee so I made her pay me in bed.
That turned her on so much she fell in love with me on the
spot.

— You're such a liar. He's psychopathic.

— Among other things, she has a nasty thing with cab
drivers. Let me give you a piece of free advice, never get
into a cab with Pamela. She has a habit of causing problems
with cab drivers, preferably Black or Puerto Rican, and the
bigger the better. The other night I was taking her over to
the porn club where she was due to perform. She was acting
crazy and nervous like she must have missed her hit or
something. Anyway when we got into the cab I saw that
there was this gigantic black Puerto Rican driving, obviously

very macho, and I knew we were in for trouble. Sure enough, first thing she does is take out a cigarette and stick her face over the back of his seat saying, not very politely, "I need a light." So the guy reaches back with his zippo and gives her a light. Which goes out in thirty seconds because she doesn't bother to puff on it, so she sticks her face over the seat again and says, "Would you mind lighting my cigarette," whereupon the driver says, "Look, lady, I'm busy driving." So she turns to me and tells me, "Tell him to give me a light," and I say, "Cool it." Then she gets on his case again till finally he says, because it's become a thing already, "What you can do is get out right here and find yourself a light," and she says, "If you get out right here you're not going to pay him." We were stopped at a red light, so I say, "Okay," get out of the cab, slam the door and walk into a subway station.

      — And what happened to her? *she asked.*

      — I don't know. I never saw her again.

come and go rutting
buffalo   the ashen w
ind   evasions of lau
ghter absences lava
fields   native song
hypothetical endocri
nology of ghosts   mu
ltifolioed many foil
ed lippings mother
no focus   not a rive
r not an ocean   foo
t wide elephant flop
intricate germinal i
nvoicing   aristocrac
y of superficial   mo
ther   mother mother

B
U
S
H

F
E
V
E
R

what's this all about if we knew we wouldn't be doing
it   let's say it's about the way the brook is flowing outside   the variations in its depth and speed which are
remarkable and sudden   let's assume we all have enough
to eat   let's assume social justice and equitable distribution of wealth   cancer even has been cured and heart
attacks controlled   in the midst of peace and social order
the soul still boils and festers   well enough cannot be left
alone and in any case   in any case there is no social justice
and famine haunts the earth   somehow armageddon
edges up despite the electronic revolution   the good life
pales the jungle moves in on utopia mother mother
mother   Freud colonized the unconscious with ambiguous results   the bush grows back with a vengeance with
vengeance   outside the brook is rising fast a storm in the
mountains   despite liberations we keep meeting ourselves in the underbrush   the talk here is about the
hundred year flood and public safety   the question is can
deliberation deliver us from liberation   the moralists of
flood control are building dikes again too late   let us however evade the central issue   taking the bull by the horns
gets you nowhere it's stronger than you   we sing instead
a song of time and place of here and now   also there and
then and where and when once upon a time   Mombassa
our story according to Kock begins with Curt under a
palm   he was reading a letter containing a check that said
find Jungle Jim   at this stage Curt was still a mercenary
adventurer journalist and part time agent   the watwat
birds were singing in the bush watwatwatwatwat and he
knew it was time to move again   he called his driver
Livingston it's time to move again he said   the bush said
Livingston is hard on a white man it gives him a hardon   a
hardon for safari and hatari and exciting dark women no
problem bwana   he said goodbye to Marylou he said he
knew it was hard it was always hard when the bush called she
said that wasn't her name   she said if it was that hard he
could stick around half an hour the bush was always wet this

time of morning   he said wet or dry was all the same to
him he was a man with bush fever   he said his fate was to
come and go he was horny as a rhino mean as a rutting
buffalo
        come and go come and go horny
        as a rhino mean as a rutting b
        uffalo the native songs the na
        tive songs he liked to hear th
        e native songs the ashen wind
here the manuscript breaks the minute penciled scribble
smudged beyond legibility an unknown number of sheets
missing from the roll of paper   such lacunae characteris-
tic throughout not only here on the blue roll but also on the
pink roll and even more so on the patterned roll that still
smells slightly of ersatz perfume   we can only speculate
on the rationale behind the missing sheets were they lost by
accident were they his means of editing   or do they
merely mean he had to wipe his ass missing sheets meaning
messy shits   preliminary examination of the manuscript
suggests that in some cases the sheets did double duty from
this we infer the deprivations of his life in jail   these
rough notes must exclude no possibilities the tragic circumstances of composition the pain the solitude the abject
conditions   the constant threat of imminent death we
feel an obligation to omit nothing on the grounds of a
privileged prudishness and yet   and yet at times the
intention is puzzling the discontinuities inexplicable one
guess might be improvisations to sustain morale   and is
this not one of the great unacknowledged themes of religion
philosophy and literature discuss this in a footnote   as to
Kock's claim to be translating into Swahili from a dialect
account of a white man who went native and led a colonial
rebellion   the legendary Curt is a legend I have not been
able to trace is possibly aimed at the politics of his jailers in
case the manuscript was discovered   and translation
from what an oral account miscellaneous stories possibly
about different people gossip   and from what language

there are twenty-eight separate languages in the jurisdiction
of Neocolonia a whole alphabet of languages mutually
incomprehensible   some spoken by as few as ten or
fifteen people wandering through the forest living on roots
and nuts and an occasional bush pig   whose speech
comes closer to total extinction with each mortality leaving
no written record suppose he's translating from one of
these   the agility and wit of the sensibility displayed says
nothing humor being the lingua franca here laughter only
after music and Swahili   or are we dealing with pure
invention desperate nonsense of a man confronting his own
fate bitter evasions of laughter translations of doom

        evasions of laughter translati
        ons of doom the native songs t
        he ashen winds blowing through
        the lava fields suggestive in
        their absences the native song

torpid   moles   nest   in   winter   might   be   a   reasonable
equivalent   though how to indicate this really signifies a
covert call to rebellion   something like the authorities
are unwary now is the time to strike   or that in social
context this does not imply a political act   on the contrary
moles mean meditation on the metaphorical level   what
the natives call darkness there is no literal translation   at
this level we are dealing with dreamtime trance and
magic   darkness is considered by the people here to be a
terrifying but benign force   it is their main stay against
depression and mortality   all the more important in that
they die like flies and are chronically depressed   dark is
the way things go along in a state of endless low grade misery   nothing going right then the moon comes out it all
turns around suddenly   suddenly everything is swell and
god is whispering in your ear how terrific you are   the
line can also translate tepid mules rest in vintage   vintage
here occurs in winter as in the first translation   though
what is winter on the equator is itself a question   also
tepid mules are not that different from moles especially tor-

pid moles   the third variant presents seemingly insur-
mountable difficulties   it is hard to see how tickled snails
vests in timber relates to one and two   yet it cannot be
ignored native lore says least likely most likely   it also
says most likely most likely completing a dark polarity   in
the dark the opposite of every true statement is also
true   such paradox is considered the heart of
darkness   such paradox is also considered trivial and
irrelevant   some commentators question my expertise
fuck them   I am the author of "Ronald Sukenick" and
other scholarly monographs   including "Herbert Melville" Herman's little known cousin   and a critical biography of Henry James's aunt   besides these are only ten-
tative notes on a preliminary translation   this story is an
excellent example of what I call corked narrative   that is
narrative that never really gets told as in the unwritten novel
of Henry James's aunt   or the untold stories of Herbert
Melville so suggestive in their absences   translating such
work is like analyzing the hypothetical endocrinology of
ghosts   under the circumstances one is forced to imagine
an optimal text as pretext   Bwana Curt on the dusty road
through the woods surrounded by torpid moles   his
unenthusiastic mule steps carefully among the hollow shells
of the vested snails   which have been tickled to death by
swarms of caterpillars spawned in a wet autumn

        the native songs the hypotheti
        cal endocrinology of ghosts th
        e text as pretext so suggestiv
        e in their absneces lava field
        s crackled porcelain ugly barr

according to the songs Curt had a trace of French accent
when he settled in the region   at that time it was a colonial outpost of Anglosaxony and that accounts for his
nickname   Zatzat was the way he sounded to the local
wasps and anglicized natives when he shrugged and said
that's that   there are those who say it was a Yiddish not a
French accent but there are those who find a Jew under

every yarmolka   those who say things like that middle
aged Jewish man tied his shoe   as if he tied it in some
peculiar rich cosmopolitan ghettoized crafty unchristian way
involving interest   but that's what you had to put up with
at the time better to be French it's not a yarmolka it's a beret
                under every yarmolka the barre
                l body the short bark traffic
                lights and tooth paste mother
                multifolioed many foiled invoi
                cing amid the native songs the
when Zatzat first got to Colonia he drank a lot women were a
problem   the only women available were too anglo for his
taste they made love but they didn't enjoy it   he began to
patronize lonely low down bars late at night listening to the
native songs   the native songs the native songs he liked
to hear the native songs   then he would spend half the
next day trying to dealcoholize his head with pills showers
vitamins coffee   it became a cycle he would waste the day
then back to the bars at night drinking local beantree beer
and cane liquor   not talking to anyone for days on end not
doing anything about finding work pissing away his
money   finally he figured what the hell gave into it got up
bleary every afternoon started writing songs himsel-
f   around then he met up with a slick dude named Dickie
Dick in Leo's Hi Life Monkey Bar   Dickie Dick was
some talker when Dickie Dick started talking the words
went snap crackle and pop   Dickie Dick had been around
he'd been everywhere from Mexico to Kokomo   Dickie
Dick had had his ups and he'd had his downs and between
the two he preferred his ups   Dickie Dick was born in
Craig but was no stranger to other Colorado metropoli like
Fort Lupton and Meeker   Dickie Dick was an American
story his family went way back some say to Plymouth
Rock   some say to criminals run out of England as inden-
tured slaves escaped to live like brutes on the Appalachian
frontier   Dickie Dick had found the way the ancestral
path it's all charm power and manipulation he told Zat-

zat   Dickie Dick was living proof of his formula an immensely successful well hard to say what   but what wasn't the point success was the point and Dickie Dick was on top vague factotum for Nutz Enterprises, Inc. a.k.a. NutzCo   so what was he doing down at Leo's Hi Life Monkey Bar with the barstool cowboys and small change torpedos   in the boozy epistemology of one A.M. Dickie Dick delegated his feelings freedom of choice here in the limbo of cigarette haze   where it couldn't hurt Dickie sighed as the folds in his cortex unkinked with the sound of snapping rubber bands   Zatzat who was sitting next to him at the bar whipped his head around watzat said Zatzat   he was completely wasted and thought he was having a fit of the D.T.s it's finally happening he said   what's finally happening said Dickie I don't know said Zatzat or Zizi as they called him for short that's the problem   I can hear cheap music clinking through your head like ice cubes and breaking glass that's the jukebox said Dickie   maybe said Zizi or maybe my ears are picking up your mind grinding gears in the higher frequencies where one can hear the nerves shift and hum   it was very interesting thought Zizi he was not a psychic but he could actually hear this man think   he could see the face go blank eyes lose focus then an audible silence a computer digesting input   what's your game said or thought Dickie Dick Zizi couldn't tell which   I blow mental guitar said or thought Zizi in this state he couldn't make fine distinctions   the squirrels were scratching through the walls making squeaky rodent noise   Zizi was ultra sensitive to this kind of thing I blow mental guitar he repeated   the trick is to keep the song going keep improvising when the song stops you die   but the squirrels are distracting he said a very strange type thought Dickie Dick   the urinals seemed very beautiful the kind of big shoulder high thrones you find in old bars   decorated by age with a network of fine cracks like Chinese crackled porcelain   the ashen winds were blowing through the lava fields and he found the decorative mode

---

93

of the urinals refreshing   the decorative mode was the
leopard coming down to drink the beautiful coat the ugly
barrel body slung from shoulders and rump   its short
bark was the single most vicious sound in the jungle
night   more frightening than sly yap insinuating moan or
giggle of hyena and wild dog   more absolute than
elephant scream or bellowing lion   it had the final author-
ity of a pistol shot the leopard barks something dies   he
had learned about the decorative mode from the jungle in
his head he had learned not to trust it   it was because of
the jungle in his head he immediately understood his new
acquaintance   who of course chose to piss in the toilet
stall he understood that yes yes   that was something
every predator in the jungle understood obsessive privacy
yes yes

> the leopard barks something di
> es no focus beyond reality eve
> rything all the time outvoicin
> g the invoicing many foiled li
> ippings bush fever untold mothe

forgetting where he was incapable of transitions his life was
becoming a series of non sequiturs   forced to wing it
wing it to the end till he was grounded to see what would
happen   there was a piece in the *Daily New* about winging it which was becoming a big if dangerous local
sport   new as opposed to news was local lingo for ongoing
stories what's new   instead of publishing bulletins the
New treated everything as the latest episode in a grand continuity   the *Daily New* was filled with seemingly irrelevant trivia it concentrated on what happened between current events   trivia was celebrated in Colonia as the substance of experience much fun was had with the journalistic
idea of the big story   a Hot Nut joined them at the bar
drummer in the group playing at Leo's   the bar was a
massive piece of blond oak from an old cowboy bar in East
Tincup Wyoming   it was riddled with real bullet holes
plugged with filler and there was an interesting story about

---

them   in Colonia filler was made cheaply from coconut shells and the man who produced it had become a millionaire   by coincidence this man was the father of the Hot Nut now standing at the bar   coincidence in Colonia was a phenomenon treated with respect and even awe   it was considered better in some way if things came about through coincidence   when something important or exciting happened people would say that was no mere matter of cause and effect   the natives dug the unforeseen newspapers ran polls expressly so people would know what was expected and not do it   the bartender was chewing out the Hot Nut may your nuts fall off he said   may they fall into the soup and be eaten by your wife so her nose sprouts coarse hairs   the Hot Nut told the bartender he was an animal but the bartender was from the south and liked animals   people in the north considered southerners animals in the north animals were the object of loathing and contempt   in the south people lived among animals and never penned them up feeling the occasional devoured villager was a small price to pay   their famous friendship with the animal kingdom was the presiding reality of southern Colonia and brought in tourists from all over the world

           multifolioed many foiled invoi
           cing mother mother traffic lig
           hts and tooth paste amid the s
           hambles no attention no focus
           everything all the time absent

the real is a matter of attention of focus   this story pays no attention has no focus   this story is everything all the time   are you grown up enough to step beyond reality   what does the tse tse fly see traffic lights and tooth paste   what the lion stalking through the high grass   or the huge rhino with his tiny dumb eyes   air conditioners and Wittgenstein Ironsides and doubleknits   this story is a jungle and the jungle is a mother this story is an appeal a cry into the darkness   under its multifolioed many foiled lippings a call into the bush   a

call like any other animal's a baby's squall asserting basic
needs   always an ongoing invocation of that capricious
capacious bitch   invoice demanding payment of what's
due never enough   bomb me muse with your big soft
bombs   sing me a song to appease the impossible wild
desire   mother mother mother said Jungle Jim and
everyone died   bush fever is the untold story that can
never be uncorked   the dark at the end of the tunnel that
makes you howl at the moon   outvoicing the invoicing of
that absent unsung song

        absent unsung song everything
        all the time no focus no reali
        ty mother consequence of varia
        bles too fine rhythm is attent
        ion if it sounds good it's bad

back to Kock or Zatzat or Zizi zizi is French for cock anyway
wisdom of language Livingston made a Kool Aid stop Kool
Aid was the national drink by government decree it was
cheap and a cabinet minister held the concession   well
you know what those roadside stands are out in the bush
natives running up from every direction to sell you trinkets
the ragged colorful costumes the bare breasted women the
eyes of the children crawling with flies they don't trouble to
brush off   ulcerated sores swollen limbs of elephantiasis
limbless beggars white eyes of the blind they were on their
way to visit the coconut filler king who was winging it up in
the mountains which rose vertically to ghostly snowcaps
floating above the equatorial plain   it was rumored that
Jungle Jim was still alive that it was a double who had died
there had always been talk of a strange alliance between
Jungle Jim and the filler king based on a morbid taste for
danger expressed in winging it both were expert
wingers   the filler king whose name was Jules Nutz was
heavily involved in the national Kool Aid concession and
everyone knew how Jungle Jim was always pushing Kool Aid
Nutz was accompanied by his teenage playmate of the year
girlfriend   mad Kewpie Slitz brewery heiress had been

singing with and fucking for the Hot Nuts when Jules stole her from his son Blue don't ask me what she was doing in Colonia some rich guy in Chicago suggested a weekend of big game hunting   by the time they got to Colonia and sobered up they had forgotten what they had come for Kewpie wandered off with the Hot Nuts in a seedy bar the guy went back to Chicago Kewpie was wacked out on pills sex and bourbon   she was so shot she couldn't even remember what she said in her last sentence she would do anything anybody suggested she was a mobile vacuum careening around in an aimless way something like a tornado   she had the virtue of normalizing the chaotic a charming if minor consequence of the collapse of the moral universe is this what John Ashbery means by the new spirit she told Nutz she preferred older men but she also preferred younger men women and animals were okay too   up there in the blue snow they were spiralling into the thermals while down here the roof leaks and the car needs to be repaired and the syntax coils and weaves dangerously like a green mamba in the bush seeking release from the tedium of prefabrication   once more Zizi recognized an impulse toward the rehabilitation of the lofty but not in the direction of the Austro-Hungarian Empire and also there was the urgent question of rhythm versus melody these are matters which linger in the space between thoughts   questions for the unrealized genius of stupor mundi whose torpor will probably finish us all but the one thing that we dare not look in the face and for good reason O Gorgon since it would kill us yet is the only thing that will finally make us happy is   on the lake not far away a million pink flamingos tinctured the acqua why shouldn't you be able to say something like that but you can't it's not that we don't believe but that we can't say it it comes to the same thing almost but not quite which is crucial   the flamingos are there nevertheless though we all know flamingos are cliche and every time Zizi passed by he would stop entranced to watch them rise from the lake like a pink mist still there are some things we need to save from the intelligence and its ravings   until its vocabulary baffles in terror and lust but then will it still be there to save us who cares nothing will save us and meantime the workers too must be allowed the visionary don't you agree   Kewpie warned him that otherwise this project would never get funding Zizi enjoyed kicking these ideas around with her she could talk about them incisively even though she had no idea what she was saying stringing together opinions of men she fucked   Zizi first met Kewpie with Blue Nutz who he met with Dickie Dick you remember who he met in Leo's Hi Life Monkey Bar Zizi walked into this restaurant where they were eating at the moment Blue had to split to cop some coke   he sat down with Kewpie and right off she dared him to make love with her at the table he had her shirt off and was playing with her exposed breasts when the head waiter came over and stepped on his foot outside she dared him to make love with her in a phone booth   he had her skirt up around her beautiful ass and pedestrians were beginning to gather around when she suddenly burst into tears and said I love my husband you aren't married Zizi reminded her she had the habit of abruptly assuming roles what would this or that feel like   this was not what he considered a real connection with a woman he told her pushing her out of the phone booth it was vacuous and immature Zizi himself had never found a role he could believe in he was himself which not only meant that he was undefined but possibly even amorphous   but is that something we have to worry about I mean can't we just leave that to our genes I mean aren't there at least some problems that will go away if we just stop paying attention to them paying attention perhaps itself being the problem   perhaps we should start paying attention to paying attention as a way of evading the central issue instead of trying to bull ahead like a horny rhinoceros soften focus well you know what those roadside stands are out in the bush natives striding stately by in gorgeous costume   women balanced straight as columns with baskets on their heads boys with the faces of young gods and girls with perfect breasts and hot eyes gazing curious one caught his glance recognized it threw back her head and laughed he decided to move north first· across the deep rift valley toward the mountains where later the guerillas would hide and rest Livingston giving a running commentary that is the police station that is the road that is the mountain maybe it was just English practice that is the what do you say the tree egg zatly the rhythm of one's sentences reflect the rhythm of one's life he told Livingston who at that moment swerved to avoid a wild dog that is the wild dog and vice versa he added the rhythm of your sentences affects the rhythm of your life now the question is what is rhythm egg zatly exactly and the answer is that rhythm is a way of paying attention without paying attention the answer is that it wells up out of the darkness the consequence of variables too fine and many for us to track that it is our way of keeping track why do I feel so happy today recording this amid the shambles of history they had begun to see the wil-debeeste moving north toward water the first thousands strung out across the rolling plains of prehistory stupendous meat rhythms for the leopards lions and cheetahs being here he told Livingston was like listening to the tune all your life and suddenly hearing the beat

> a way of paying attention with
> out paying if you know the way
> it's not the way a streak of q
> uicksilver it is not a river i
> t is not an ocean what is not

suddenly all those numbers you've been running on yourself seem very thin when you hear the cadence underneath com-ing back again and again after a while you completely ignore the melody the melody is just an excuse a whole new lan-guage emerges in which at first you are capable of only gross distinctions and even to get that far takes a lot of nerve moving beyond taste far beyond belles lettres and the embroidery of thought where everything is impossible everything you've done and everything you intended to do and only one criteria if it sounds good it's bad if it sounds bad at least you're still alive and that's not much help either and so evasion becomes your weapon avoiding all familiar paths if you know the way it's not the way calculated disruption followed by incalculable vapidity quickly degenerating into the merely silly and then toss in a few offensive banalities just to make sure you are judged wanting especially by your-self and then the important question arises wanting what my advice is go on immediately to another topic something must be wrong if you have to kill yourself every time you want to come to life the only solution is to keep a record so that next time it will be graceful civilized and pretty when of course it will no longer be *a propos* but maybe at least then the pro-cess will be a little more familiar and if that is no comfort whatever to you at least it may keep the others from too quickly consigning you to oblivion and may even help keep you out of jail or anyway Margaritaville

        and we stopped
        at a pool
        halfway up the mountain
        the silence between
        water dripping
        from the ledge
        filled my body
        like a gong

one morning he woke up before dawn   striped muzzle of zebra chomping grass at tent flap   startled herd through thin light horse scared galloping   in the distance mean cape buffalo mooing like cows   the gazelle lifting their heads were nervous   maribou storks on dead branches flopped heavy wings   the pastoral of prehistory spread out on the plains   the calm and gorgeous giraffe paced by in slow motion   calling into question the shambles of his-tory

---

and we stopped
at a pool
halfway up the mountain
the water dripping
water dripping
from the ledge
measured silence
into time

there's a lot to be said for history he told Livingston it allows
for the accumulation of capital   time is a mercantile
invention as a rhythm it's totally boring it cancels out but it's
powerful   it all goes back to narrative a Jewish invention
and then and then and then and   if money is a kind of
poetry credit is a kind of fiction the plot of Jewish time
against Christian eternity   back in America we've purifi
ed time to a streak of quicksilver so fine it doesn't even
exist   it was a mistake trying to escape time only when
you become it does it cancel out   anyway you are it
everything is it what is not time I ask you this opens possibilities   I mean it is not as if you were floating along on
the river of time watching matter shore by   it is not a
river it is an ocean it is not an ocean it has no coasts say a
boundless tide   but within it vast currents spirals eddies
twists curlicues vibrations counterpoints quavers syn-
copations   what do we do when a form restrains our intelligence get rid of it I say so with history   the problem no
longer accumulation of capital but distribution of resour-
ces   and does chronology exist at the speed of light or do
we get patterns of information   as with the cosmos so
with the quanta sequence without chronology pre-
vails   we have grown beyond history as already religion
we now move from history to story itself

           it is not a river it is not an
           ocean what is not the poetry o
           f absence evasion silence and
           foot wide elephant flop this s

tream of pure nothing interrup
and here the boring powerful drive of progress and the subtle mysterious rhythms of supposedly timeless tribal life fos-
silized as heaven in our theologies beget glorious bastards of
form as we meditate the unplanned parenthood of the mes-
siah   but who can say what story is these days there's no
longer any question of continuity or if continuity then continuity reduced to inescapable sequence of discontinuous
fragments which shows at least that life goes on which is the
point   and maybe that's what story is a tuning of the
nerves to the score of life in all its irreducible twists and
possibilities contained in the prophetic multiplicity of language in the wisdom of its evasions our only salvation   and so Kock moves from the poetry of pure fact to
the poetry of thought to the poetry of absence evasion and
silence also known as prayer while seeming to move
nowhere at all in the dreamtime of weird hyrax call and foot
wide elephant flop   in these rhythms we sense the work-
ings of an occult system vital and irrelevant having to do no
doubt with the organization of his day the arrangement of
objects in his cell rush and ebb of pain anguish maintenance
of temporary self inflicted schizophrenia   it may even be
that Kock's interest in Zizi and mine in Kock has to do with
the discovery of this system I mean what is the area of discourse here my hypothesis is that Kock isn't writing this at
all it's actually composed by a Chino in the next cell   this
fellow named Dong Wang a Chinese Mexican revolutionary
raised in Texas and trained in Cuba is telling the story of Zizi
by tapping in code on the wall though it's a code Kock is not
certain he understands in fact he's not even certain it's a
code   maybe he's just trying to pick a hole in the wall or
tapping a tune to keep himself sane or beating out his brains
or counting sheep or figuring out the square root of pi or
calculating his days left in confinement or simply venting
nervous energy   the result is finally nobody is sure who is
making up what or what it is that's being made up and on the
basis of what we only know that somebody is making some-

thing up I mean we don't just sit here and watch phenomena
go by with a blank moronic stare   and we know too that
the ability to do this is in some mysterious way that for some
reason nobody is willing to acknowledge probably for fear of
mitigating its magic or maybe enhancing it depending very
potent in face of the reality principle   or anyway those in
power think so Khrushchev and the painters for example or
Martin Luther King or why is Dong Wang in jail for publiciz-
ing certain abstract and probably fallacious political theories
because they encode general fears and expectations   and
an attitude toward them a tone which implies a way of coping
let us try to reduce all mysteries to a minimum when Cecil
Taylor taps out a tune he is not merely meditating amuse-
ment for the millions there is a rhetoric of rhythm we tend to
tune out   also there are secrets implied in polyps and
colloids infarctation and candelabra banalities and flats each
one of these a tiny novel awaiting germination pure thought
however has no sound no rhythm no meaning only movement through time   the rest comes in as interference as
resistance as assertion of being the first consequence is
rhythm you have this stream of pure nothing interrupted by
intermittent beeps of pure something this is about as basic as
I can get said Zizi said Dong Wang said Kock   egg zatly
said Livingston or so Kock interpreted Dong Wang's intermittent tapping on the wall encoding the biography of Zizi
which for all Kock knew might have been pure invention in a
code which might not even be a code so that Kock despite
himself might be making it all up   making what all up
well that's what he's making up what's what he's making
what he's making up what kind of tree is that Zizi asked
Livingston Livingston shrugged you can call that kind of tree
anything you want he said Zizi thought he was going to faint
          beeps of pure something call t
          hat tree anything subliminal d
          ead dogs payoff of intricate g
          erminal invoicing an intellige
          nce of movement the aristocrac

first of all Zizi wasn't even sure what he was looking for of course he was looking for Jungle Jim   but who was Jungle Jim the revolutionary leader of an international death cult but wasn't that contradiction   but a contradiction from an ex adman who invented subliminal dead dogs in liquor advertising is pure surface   but surface is exactly where it's at exfoliation being the complex sensational payoff of intricate germinal invoicing   now we know and the long history of the soul suddenly collapses like the exploding smokestack in *Blood of a Poet*   sudden tie-in with one of Jim's reported sermons entitled the soul essence or abcess after screwing Kewpie Slitz   Jules Nutz decided to share her with Jungle Jim in a bondage and humiliation scene her vivacity astonished them   she took the initiative started inventing their fantasies before they had a chance to have them leaving them mired in reality   made them think twice about thinking twice converted them to a discipline of thoughtlessness yet she wasn't dumb   an intelligence of movement gesture tact with space that argued the aristoc-racy of the superficial and made fun of Beethoven   this pretty young ignoramus had them by the balls and they loved it who was using who in the lava fields of the soul

the aristocracy of the superfi
cial as complex sensational pa
yoff of intricate germinal inv
oicing increased consciousness
of increased unconsciousness m

it was Dickie Dick who took her to the coast   relations between Zizi and Lala were too absurd   they were beyond getting along they just weren't making contact   it figured that Lala and Dickie would connect   it was a case of Jewish princess meeting Wasp aristocrat   neither were either but both had that tone   both had an idea of the good life   his involved success and power hers culti-vation and liberal politics   as opposed to Zizi's romantic revolutionary posturing   which as he knew could only land him in prison   if not the prison of one side then that of the other   having neither social base nor ideological rationale he was left with good impulses   up on the mountain things were a lot simpler   Nutz believed effi cient exploitation equaled social good   and if it didn't fuck you you could quote him on that   Kewpie Slitz was a highly trained consumer sent out by the CIA   these types usually rich young women were programmed to use up things and people   they were more efficient than technological warfare and had little else to do   they even developed a certain charm if you didn't think too much about what it was   people were vaguely bothered by Dick's peculiar odor but suppressed it   one time he invited Zizi home where the smell was impossible to ignore   Zizi was about to ask when Dickie's eyes snapped into a fixed stare   he began drooling and slavering and headed for the kitchen entranced   the kitchen was filled with open cans of putrid festering garbage   emitting strange animal growls Dickie threw himself on a maggoty can   grasping the sides he lapped and crunched doglike until he was sated   then sighing he wiped his mouth with his sleeve and chose a bottle from the wine rack   a 1976 *Morgon* he said rather smoky but flatters a piquante cuisine   Jungle Jim though knew everyone's cards and had the strongest hand   had the strongest hand and knew it wasn't worth shit   and maybe that's why Jungle Jim had the strongest hand   Jim had a strong following of lem- mings all over the world   they were a potent political force threatening suicide if provoked   no regime wanted all those corpses to explain at the U.N.   dead bodies were bad press and bad business especially for tourism   foreign investors would get the image of an unstable labor force   workers popping themselves off at the factory worse than strikes   a few self immolations were enough to get the ministers on the phone   if not he soon had them diving off buildings out of planes   any- thing to make a mess blowing their brains out in front of the palace   eviscerating themselves at gala performances of the opera   it was the end of ideology what these people believed in was dying   it gave everything they did a kind of edge their motto was joy and death   for young renegades from the middle class it provided a final *frisson*   and an ultimate power trip if you don't give me what I want I'll kill myself   for the impoverished and oppressed it provided an instant solution   looking into the happy eyes of these clones converted you instantly to sadness   now the organization was busy colonializing underdeveloped areas   the heart of darkness was always an export in partnership with types like Nutz   in Colonia though people had a different feeling about the incomprehensible   mystery was subtle susceptible to fine distinctions exhilarating contradictions   people here would find a benign side to the mystery of the lemming   nature's response to overcopulation leading to overpopulation   incidentally explaining the oft observed connection of love with death   confirming Lala's theory that love was nature's anesthetic for reproduction   by which criterion Zizi and Lala were certainly no longer in love   relations like barbed wire prevailed when they were together   Zizi's theory was that increased consciousness included increased unconsciousness   that is increased consciousness of increased unconsciousness   he thought if consciousness left out unconsciousness it was unconscious   example when he found his ring and watch in the hotel she disappeared   the symbolism of that was not something he was unconscious of   and she didn't know about it it seemed to Zizi the world was unconscious   unconscious but not inert that is it was a live unconsciousness   that the unconsciousness of things of events was wise and vital   vital even when destructive alive with its own kind of economy   Jungle Jim's worship of darkness as malign as death was a mistake mother   you do not find unconsciousness by losing consciousness *au contraire*   one was part of the other ignorance of this can cause great despair

in	life	unbearably	time
any	was	dismal	to
case	getting	blocked	move

| but | | | where |

the cats were in the chambers
when the feather merchant show
ed up saying i got something t
hat will tickle you but the ma
jor came in and everybody had
to shape up then a mad Rumania
n rescued the situation using
his secret code calling all va
mpires so before you know it e
veryone was having a good time
again and a good thing too bec
ause Zizi was about to reach f
or the phone to call Dr. O and
you know what that means no we
ll make a note to make a footn
ote meanwhile the situation wa
s really pissing Lala off Zizi
always forgot what a drag it w
as to see her after twenty fou
r hours his body started to ac
he then went numb and for the
rest of the time it was total
rigor mortis she was a weird c
ombination of mischievous infa
nt and grouchy granma everythi
ng in between left out why cou
ld he never remember this sent
imentality leads to amnesia he
could hardly wait for Dickie D
ick to come and take her to th
e coast he was thinking of sen
ding him a fucking telegram wh
at Zizi wanted was a bottle of
JD a pack of Gauloise some lou
d music a twentyone year old g
irl a few joints a little coca
ine wouldn't hurt either what

Zizi wanted was to wake up in the morning with an awful hang over next to a pretty girl he didn't know very well who also had an awful hangover both of them completely demerded and k nowing they would feel happy a nd relaxed after a nice breakf ast which they would have in s ome terrible place called Panc ake Palace drop her off come h ome take a big shit write fift een letters humming to himself nodding all *right* all *right* Mr. Feelgood of course this is onl y half the story completely on esided but if you want the oth er side ask her

don't trust what he says but h ow he says it and don't trust how he says it but the rhythm of how he says it in their cas e telling about it the rhythms would be a song of slow disint egration ending with the ambig uous blessings of entropy the irrelevance of what was said p art of the advancing slackness finally moving so far apart th at even gravity relinquishes t he gravity of gathering time th at is that accumulates in prop ortion to time spent together giving way to levity then to o utright foolishness which has its survival value through a p rocess of decay accelerated by

---

109

the corporate intervention of
Dickie Dick and NutzCo last bl
ast of white wind sending him
to the mountains her to the co
ast according to the requireme
nts of a force itself without
substance Dickie Dick and Kewp
ie Slitz vacuums of pure energ
y the spiritual equivalent of
campaign rhetoric I hear Ameri
ca slinging and yet is it not
possible that as we gain one k
ind of energy we lose another
and vice versa on the assumpti
on that the flux is no mere op
en ended leak like leak to whe
re but a see-saw so tracing th
is gradual decline if you have
the guts to ride it may when y
ou are most down put you in th
e position of maximum potential
energy tragedy contains such c
ontradictions but let us not g
uilt the silly since what she
wants is not so very different
from what he wants they just c
an't give it to one another an
ymore it seems just another Am
erican story the past thrown o
verboard and bobbing away in t
heir wake history behind them
nothing ahead but pure time an
d space in between

and then

they were driving along t
he lip of despair the edg
e of Kikiyu country and d

own the escarpment to whe
re the Masai herd their h
ump necked long eared cat
tle and then they were dr
iving through a flat coun
try of low thorn trees hi
gh hills rising on every
side mountains in the dis
tance to the right numero
us gazelle giraffe every
where zebra and the first
thousands of wildebeeste
strung out along the hill
s vanguard of the vast se
asonal move toward water
leaving the tarmac for ro
cky gravel track red dust
coating everything in a v
ery bad mood wondering w
hat the hell was the point
of all this and then they
got their second flat tir
e in twenty minutes and t
hey got out and Livingsto
n looked around at the gr
ass and low bush and said
I am used to changing the
tire while you are used t
o watching for lion izzen
tit and Zizi went sure ha
h hah and started hamming
it up with the binos whil
e Livingston puts on seco
nd spare and they got bac
k in flat out of spares i
n the middle of nowhere a
nd Zizi said well at leas

t we weren't attacked by any lions hah hah and at that very moment Livingst on shrieked to a stop sid eways around a curve to a void four lions on the ro ad a big female and three mostly grown cubs she sta red at the car with big y ellow eyes then swung her head back toward the bush she is very serious said Livingston as they walked into the bush they are ve ry hungry said Livingston a half mile down the road they meet two small Masai boys herding goats wearin g tunics to bellybuttons otherwise naked Jambo Liv ingston said simba pointi ng back up the road the b igger of the two about ni ne shook a club he was ca rving saying something in his language I am going t o kill simba with my club Livingston translates hah hah very cute I said late r Livingston told him tha t's what Masai boys do fo r their bar mitzvah kill a lion with a club so the n of course Zizi got into an old leech gatherer hea d shamed out of depressio n nothing like a hungry w ild lion on the road for tonic effect or for that matter a grown teenage Ma sai warrior out in the bu sh with club spear hennae d hair and a mean juvenil e delinquent look in his eye

Livingston who was a Kikuyu considered th e Masai uncivilized first of all they sm elled bad they were cattle thieves they did nothing but foll ow the cows and get drunk they made thei r women do all the w ork they were unchri stian and superstiti ous they didn't care about money they ref used to market their cattle they grazed o n illegal land Zizi was travelling at a time when everything was unstable tribal fights second only t o rebellious agitati on against the colon ial regime in fact t hough no one realize d it absolutely Colo nia was already on t he other side of the

their relation was g oing through some fi nal if not quite ack nowledged transition a lot of pain would twist down the drain here on the other si de of the equator in the opposite directi

113

on before they would be willing to accept the inevitable but f or the time being th ey had split into tw o separate columns s he heading for the b eaches of the Indian Ocean he into the bu sh and this was one of the reasons for h is case of bush feve r though it was a di sease to which he ha d always been highly vulnerable he knew t he end was in sight when they started ar guing about money th at's always the fina l throe there was no thing so sad and dep ressing as those day s nothing so down so full of sullen silen ce breaking in anger at any provocation a nd anything was prov ocation waking up in the morning thinking about broken backs a nd the best age to c ommit suicide so he decided to commit hi mself instead to joy rather than happines s excitement rather divide sliding inevi tably toward transit ion to Neocolonia i.e. foreign exploitation partly replaced by n ative exploitation i t would take years a nd a lot of blood to confirm the situatio n but let us not be cynical Neocolonia w as a big step ahead yet so short of gene ral expectations wit h its critics in pri son including writer s and intellectuals with its political a ssassinations domina tion by one tribe of the other eighty per cent business ripoff s in collusion with foreign capital it w as like a bad parody of home even the ele phants were not exem pt threatened by ext inction through the illegal ivory trade with the collusion o f high officials who at the same time wer e passing laws autho rizing summary execu tion of poachers tho ugh this reduced thr

than stability anywa
y he had always beli
eved in a safari vie
w of life a journey
on which you might r
est but never stop w
here nothing was cer
tain not even destin
ation and lots of su
rprises good and bad
and the incertitudes
of travel become a
prosody of experienc
e a measure of ident
ity old American plo
y for lack of other
measure yet who know
s though well aware
at the end of the ro
ad Jim Slitz Nutz an
d all that stands fo
r mother mother moth
er sometimes Zizi th
ought it might be be
st for all of. us to
go back to our first
wives husbands lover
s high school crushe
s nursemaids whateve
r and start all over
again back to the Ga
rden of Eden typical
American nostalgia f
or purity for death
that is death the cl
ean slate the new st
art the frontier as

ough recognition of
animal watching as t
he country's main in
dustry thus no more
animals no more tour
ists

salvation safari hat
ari drugs and licquo
r skulls and dead do
gs in whisky ads

    the important thing is a feeling
    the important thing is to keep it open
    the important thing is to evade connections
    the important thing is to arrest development
    the important thing is not to look back
    the important thing is to think at the edge
    the important thing is to leave it behind
    the important thing is to avoid the beautiful
    the important thing is to butcher the harmonious
    the important thing is to jerk off good taste
    the important thing is to parenthesize signification
    the important thing is to bracket and sack it
    the important thing is to love it and shove it
    the important thing is to outthink premeditation
    the important thing is to pursue the continuum
    the important thing is a beat
    the important thing is to annihilate the important thing

    how all day
    the wildebeeste strung through the hills
    endless
    cheetahs lions vultures following
    dumb clumsy
    stunning in their numbers

    how at evening
    elephants charging out of the forest
    blaring
    cleared the buffalo from the waterhole

            trunks lifted
            how his feelings had shrunk

include everything
how the crickets in the grass under the zebras
        sounded like the gonging of bells
how the elephant was very angry
        when he flapped his ears
how the vervet monkey
        had bright blue balls
how the lizard
        walked straight up the wall
how the minimum
        is included in the maximum

there's a lot to
                be said for the
                                ugly and stupid the
energy there as
                Sonny Barger the
                                point to be as re
pulsive as possible
                so here's to
                                you Sid Vicious
                                the ragged the jagged
                                the half baked
                                is most delicious

                                                Beethoven
among the elephants
                        Beethoven in the jungle
                                                Beethoven
boogies with bulbuls

Beethoven appeasing wart hogs

Beethoven pleasing the hippopotamus

Beethoven
boring the rhinoceros

Beethoven goes to a Masai
cattle raid

Beethoven watching a flamingo flap

Beethoven amazed at the hyrax call

Beethoven
reacts to the oryx horn

Beethoven blinks at the vulture dance

Beethoven menaced by mild monkeys

Beethoven
protests the turaco's squawk

Beethoven gawks as the ibis soars

Beethoven blubbers in Bantu


```
            Z
            i
      Z i Z i Z
            i
            Z


    L
    a
    L  L
  L a L a
      L
  L a L a
```

```
                l
    disintegration of
                b
                e
                r
                jackal
                l

                e
                p              w
                history's  music
                s h            l
                  r            d
                  u
                  s            d
                  t            o
                               g
                  o
                  f

                  b
                  l
                  a
                dark of bush
                e              e
                               r
                               d


                       s
                       w
                    terminal olduvai turkana express
                       l                          n
                       l                          o
            maribou stork                         l
                                                  a

                                                  g
                                                  a
                                               hyena
```

great rift

                      opens

scavengers   mother

                      define

mother   carrion

                      mother

vulture   mother

                      defines

mother   carcass

                      mother

mother   mother

mother   mother

                      mother

a dissa and a data
it's what's in betwee
n that counts recidi
vist wretch   everyth
ing began turning in
to everything   sizzl

ed tires through dar
k filthy back street
s intimidated the se
miconductors extenua
ting the line betwee
n monday and oblivio
n   prepubescent in
sawyerish complicity
boom

END OF ENDLESS SHORT STORY

We're all walking corpses, he said. Nicht wahr? So what's the big deal. Life is not da capo. Pas de la tête. Del cuerpo. That's the truth, buddy. Daverro? We were floating down the river on a marble slab a talkin about a dissa and a data. We had plenty of data but not enough dissa. Whatsa dissa? Ahma gonna tella you. Foist of all when you go to sleep and you dream you gotta dissa. When you dream you no gotta data you gotta dissa. Capish? Den inna oily mawnin you gotta more dissa den inna milaladay, inna oily mawnin an late at night. Inna milaladay ya gotta lotta data, so where's it getcha? You no spik spic you spik a good Americano Englitch. Bueno, pero death no drink Cafe Bustelo, death speak Esperanto cha-cha-cha. De ole Brooklyn Dodgers dey hadda dissa, da Yankees dey hadda data ceptin mebbe Lou Gehrig he hadda dissa. Mick Jagger got data Billie Holiday had dissa. Romans data Greeks dissa. American data Italian dissa. You begin to dig?

Abei gezunt, said his companion. He had the fishing line between his toes off the end of the marble slab. The hook was baited with stones because he was after cement fish. I don't mean to be impolite but what's all this dissa horse dookie. You talk funny.

Dissa, responded his interlocutor. Disappointment. Disafiliation. Dissociation. Dissatisfaction. Disaccord. I talk funny because language is full of lies. You have to make it tell the truth. You have to crack it open. Krack! Zo.

Careful you'll chip the raft, said Hardy Crapp. And besides what's so good about dissa, I mean frankly I don't see it. Sounds like a sad song to me. He pulled up a small plaster goldfish and threw it back.

Eggs ackly, said I. P. Daly. Disastrous. We discern, we disapprove, we discourse, we dissent, we disdain, we dissemble, we dissipate, we disembody, we disappear. Discontinuity. Dis. Dissolution. Discouraging. Despair.

You leave me speechless, said Crapp.

There are over four hundred and fifty thousand words in the language, said Daly. Pick one.

Only four hundred fifty thousand? aksed Crapp. His rod was bent almost double with the weight of a granite carp.

Not counting slang, scientific designations, coinages, regionalisms, foreign words, ethnic variations, baby talk, wordplay, mumbling and nonsense. That adds several million more, said Daly, unzipping his pants and taking a piss off the edge of the raft. But only two of them are important.

Which two? aksed Crapp. He netted the granite carp and pulled it flopping onto the marble slab where it made a sound like ten billiard games. It was smooth and grey and he split its head open with a chisel and dropped it into his creel.

The first one begins with b and ends with h and travels by subway.

Which line?

I.R.T.

And the second?

Also ends with h but starts with d. And in between you eat.

By which we conclude?

That the end is always the same and the beginning doesn't matter. It's what's in between that counts.

You're dying?

It's just that my brain is granulated by the voyage. Yours is turning to gravel.

That may be, mused Crapp. I sound like marracas when I shake my head. A metal duck whistled overhead.

They tossed a few matzo balls back and forth for a while.
Thoughtfully.

Wawa, I. P. Daly said.

What are you trying to get at? aksed Hardy Crapp.

Peepee. Doodoo. Caca.

Yes. Of course. The caca birds are due to peep. I have
been trying to keep that possibility foremost. I have been
trying to suggest it to you by implication, by explication, by
more or less precise analysis of the structure, indeed
through deconstruction of the omnipresent conifers along
the banks which you choose to ignore concentrating instead
on the ooze of recombinant honeys while I'm up before
dawn every morning alerted by the glistening drill bit of the
ladderbacked jackhammer, you recidivist wretch. I hope
you brought lunch.

Tu parle, said I. P. Daly. Yet any turkey who understands how to say vector can find a position in the high
echelons of anything these days. Use vector and parameter
in the same sentence and they make you a prince of
industry. Then they feed you to the dogs howling at the edge
of town. It's called urban slough.

Today is garbage day, said Hardy Crapp. Don't
forget to throw out the garbage.

I'll throw it out this evening when the catfish call.
When they crawl up from the muddy belly of the great
brown serpent. When they wave their whiskers and belch
carrion at the unsuspecting secretaries. When they march
through the cemeteries. When they knife toward the raft
that wallows in the water like a patient on an operating table
waving terrible garage door openers. That's when I'll throw
out the garbage, said I. P. Daly.

Do it, said Hardy Crapp. Say, there's Tara Titzov
waving from shore.

She's with Wun Hung Lo! exclaimed I. P. Daly.

(Hm) thought Hardy Crapp (what's she doing with
Wun Hung Lo?).

(Hm) thought I. P. Daly (what's she doing with Wun

Hung Lo?).

What do you suppose she's doing with Lo? aksed Crapp.

I was wondering the same thing, said Daly.

Let's get stoned and go ashore, said Crapp.

Right on, said Daly.

Each picked up a stone and cocked his arm.

Go! yelled Crapp. Each hurled his stone at the other's head, each staggered and started reeling around the raft.

Wow, mumbled Daly. I'm really blasted. Too much. Mom always told me to stay away from the hard stuff.

Shit, said Crapp, clutching his head. I'm *really* fucked up. That's strong stuff. What are we doing, marble?

I used the granite carp, said Daly.

They turned the raft in to shore. It was autumn and the trees were turning. They were turning colors you wouldn't believe so why bother mentioning them. Except to say they were unbelievable. They couldn't have been real. Let us all be friends. Let us all forgive one another and pat one another on the back. Let us put our arms around one another's shoulders and shed tears together. Let us feel sorry for one another. Have mercy. It will all wash away. With the colors with the leaves with the trees with the river itself we are all traveling on that washes itself away. With the river of belief which is hope which is words that wash themselves clean have mercy. Like the racoons washing their berries on the banks which themselves will wash away. Have mercy have mercy have mercy. That was what I. P. Daly was thinking as the marble slab drifted gently into shore. And that was more or less Hardy Crapp's frame of mind too as the slab nuzzled the muddy bank, snagged a resting place and held on. By the time they got up onto the bank Lo had turned into a racoon and birds were coming out of his mouth. Each bird appeared on his lower lip, peered around and leaped into the air unfurling into a colorful symbol of mutability, metamorphosing quickly into a wide variety of dissa and data. In fact, blimey! everything began turning into everything else. The trees turned into snow sculptures and the fish turned into skaters skating on the icy river to a Strauss waltz. The blue sky turned grey and the air turned into tinsel and Tara Titzov, before they even had time for a kiss on the cheek, turned into a yurt, which they entered, building a fire of dried yak dung to keep warm. The wind howled outside and the mournful sound made them nostalgic and cozy. Their thoughts had a comfortable monotony that seemed to keep pace with the metronome of the windshield wipers and when they tuned in a talk show they heard themselves talking about the good old days with I. Bitchakokoff the M.C.

Do you remember how we were afraid of everything then? aksed Crapp.

Terrified, replied Daly. What were we not terrified of?

We were not terrified of ice cream cones, suggested Crapp.

No, we were definitely not terrified of ice cream cones, acquiesced Daly. At least very probably not. But perhaps we liked them too much?

Life is never perfect, demurred Crapp. And if it were what would you do? You very well might hang yourself.

Now, yes, responded Daly. But then. Then I remember long perfect days with sunny skies, plenty to eat and lots of warm flesh to boot.

To boot?

To boot if you were in an ugly mood or to lick and fondle if so desired and by it to be fondled and licked. Amen.

Amen. What else were we not terrified of?

Very little. You could have counted it on the fingers of one hand. If you were not terrified of fingers.

Were you terrified of god? asked I. Bitchakokoff.

Oh yes, answered Daly. We were certainly terrified of god. And ladies. Now we are not terrified of god because god is dead thank god. According to Nietzsche.

And so is Nietzsche, put in Crapp. Now we are terrified of death. Who next?

And what about ladies? asked Bitchakokoff.

Ladies are still alive, answered Daly.

All of them? asked Bitchakokoff.

No. Some are dead and some are alive.

How do you explain that? asked Bitchakokoff.

I can explain almost everything else but that's one thing I can't explain, answered Daly.

Almost everyone can explain almost everything else, complained Bitchakokoff. If someone could explain death nobody would need to explain everything else.

They were driving down the frozen river, which had turned into a superhighway, in the yurt, which had turned into a Datsun Z. As they zipped along the pike the tires sizzled on the asphalt with a sound like zzzzzzz making them drowsy and as they drove each had dozens of dreams. I. P. Daly dreamed that he lived in a place called Vista Point, on Frontage Road. It was a modest neighborhood of backyards and lawns and window boxes and clotheslines and pies cooling on window sills and pussycats among peach trees and milk bottles on the porch and paper boys on bicycles and old washing machines rusting at the back door and pale people in pajamas picking tomatoes in the après midi and joes in long johns jamming on late night guitars and bottled fetuses sold at permanent garage sales and rotting car carcasses parked on shoulders and molested children sobbing in closets and bodies long since buried in victory gardens pushing up the produce and pimpled pimps peddling poxy tarts and drunks puking against street lights on cold starry nights o lord.

The hitchiker on the side of the road turned out to be Seymour Hare, Crapp's attorney. He was carrying his cat, Nuage, trying to keep it warm. What are you doing out here at night all alone like a stranger? aksed Crapp.

Every now and then I get a strong urge to be alone, explained Seymour Hare. Alone like Greta Garbo or J. D.

Salinger. Then I take my cat Nuage and wander lonely as a cloud or even lonely as a crowd through the dark, filthy back streets at the edge of town, hoping to stumble across my mother or my ex-wife. I never have, not to date, but if I did I would extend a hand, a helping hand, and help them up, and brush them off, and give them moral support and maybe a few dollars. Then I would give Nuage a little milk and myself take a pull on my pint of whisky, Nuage my only friend. Then I would compose a prose poem on the situation, and if that didn't help I'd stick out my thumb and start hitching and be picked up by I. P. Daly and Hardy Crapp driving in a Datsun Z, Crapp behind the wheel.

Sho nuff, said Crapp, popping clutch and peeling out. Zoom, zum, zoom, he yelled. Zum, zoom, zum. Zum golly golly golly, zum golly golly. Nuage started doing a little dance on the back seat. Then Crapp switched to Hatikvah and Nuage joined in, weeping. Nuage was a Jewish cat, which caused Hare many problems. First of all it was hard to find kosher cat food. Second of all he couldn't feed her canned food and milk at the same meal, so he was always going around with his jacket pockets full of dry food. Hare was Irish. He didn't know how he ended up with a Jewish cat, when he got her as a kitten he thought she was a Persian, grey and furry, but during her second year she grew a very long nose and went into heat. She got insulted when Hare referred to her as a Persian. Persians were Iranians, she said, and Iranians were Moslems. I forgot to say, she was a rabid Zionist. She was always making remarks like, Next year in Jerusalem. She would grudgingly accept Hare's attentions at the end of the day, his petting his bits of tuna or nip. But, she would add, Next year in Jerusalem. Hare considered her haughty, especially for a cat, but what really nibbled at him was the suspicion she was smarter than he was. He was always paranoid she was manipulating him. Especially about finding her a Jewish mate. A Jewish mate! Holy shit, how many Jewish cats were there in the world anyway? Damn few. And how the hell was he supposed to tell, go around with a magnifying glass to see if they were circumcized? Meanwhile, every time she went into heat she got real cranky and her nose grew a little bit too, it seemed to Seymour Hare.

And so the world zipped by, with its usual mixture of lethal certitude and aggravating confusion. Eyes ablaze, the rearing stallions of Dis intimidated the semiconductors while the grimy sprawl of the Fine Can Company added its touch of grandeur to the Brooklyn waterfront. The sleepy trio of the car pool stole last sips from their steaming thermoses as their battered but eager old Mustang snorted past the gate house, ignoring the ancient guardian's elaborate wave of the arm and cry of, Et voila, Messieurs! In any case they didn't understand Froganese, Brooklyn boys all, a little Italian, a little Yiddish maybe and that's it. They parked the heap, punched the clock, Hare, Daly, Crapp along with all the other poor suckers and shuffled to their places on the line, already looking forward to the ten o'clock break and the Baby Ruth and the powdered coffee from the machines, knowing this is how it always ended up for them no matter who won the wars. This is where, for them, the deep, brown mysterious river had been leading, led, would always lead, the great brown river of shit, as Hardy Crapp liked to call it. To the mine shafts, to the auto plants, to the janitorial services, to the garbage dumps, the mighty industrial army of America marching along, its head lifted high to keep its nose out of the shit. Still, it was true the boys on the Fine line took a pathetic pride in the product of their eight hours. A Fine Can is a fine can, went the motto of the company. And besides the crooked union was cooperating with management on a speed-up system rewarding the foolhardy and attenuating the fine line between Monday and oblivion. These people, they were not interested in getting ahead because there was nothing ahead. The only thing that ever got ahead was the assembly line if they slowed down. The most they could ever hope to do was keep up. They were not interested in progress because there was no progress. They were not interested in salvation because there was no salvation. They were interested maybe in getting enough money together to open a bar some day or in moving down to Daytona Beach and living in a trailer park. I. P. Daly knew this was where it all ended for him, brain granulated by voyage, words washed clean of hope. Low level of organization reflected by his mutilated companions avoiding imposition of zeitgeist. All there, Tara Titzov, Red Angel of the Apocalypse, heavy scepticism of Wun Hung Lo, the acerbly analytical I. Bitchakokoff, and the others, prepubescent in their sawyerish complicity with the yellow stream of the quotidian. Sullen rebels against the dictionary. Insurgents of the impossible, princes of foolishness, boogalooing to the unboogalooable. Specialists of flat refusal. I am going nowhere and I want to go nowhere, nowhere is where I want to go, sung Lo, accompanied by Bitchakokoff on the electric washboard, while Titzov paraded with a placard that read, We protest tits and pubic hair. Wun Hung Lo hung around and heckled. Hey goilie, donchiz wanna play docta wit me no maw? You fool you, remarked Bitchakokoff. That won't help. Nothing helps.

Suddenly the luminescent ghost of Jim Morrison floated down from the ceiling, singing in his hollow sexy voice. This is the end. My only friend the end.

Boom, said Crapp. Just like that. Boom.

The End of the Endless Short Story, Continued

They were all headed to the Starlite Roof for the big bar mitzvah in the sky. Bitchakokoff sharpened the herrings. Today the world is filled with data, even the Dis of dissa doubles as data. Better dissaway den dataway. Drunk with chaos, as the man sez. Leaves litter lawn. Front fence falling forward. Weeping willow wants Wilkie. Squirrels squawk in square. Clotheslines cross-cross creation. Busses barge past barrooms. Mailmen march moodily many Mondays, most mean it, moan. Houses hint horrendous haunts. Dummies dig dikes, deranged dogs. Grimy greasers grin at gringos. Nosey neighbors, not nice, nibble nasties. Panting puppies piss in the park. Real rats roam. Tacky todays topple terrible tomorrows. Victors win, ecstatic, yearn for zilch.

Messiaen's "Quartet For the End of Time," composed in a Nazi concentration camp, was terminal, said Hardy Crapp.

Right, said I. P. Daly, but the end of one time is always the beginning of another kind of time. And who knows what the mailman may bring?

the target is poetry
wordbombs   the mail
man of fate   suck blu
b   fishfood again

P   a postcard from THE ENDLESS SHORT STORY. THE ENDLESS SHORT
O   STORY has a secret ambition it wants to write The Great Amer
S   ican Postcard. These are some of the requirements for The
T   Great American Postcard it has to have a Great Character.
    It has to have an All Encompassing Plot. It has to be Signific
C   ant and easy to read. It should be Serious but not so seri
A   ous as to make us feel bad. It has to Make a Short Story
R   Long. It has to have Fire Thrust Impact Tension and Vivid
D   Descriptions. The ESS knows it can do it it knows that insid
    e its prosy exterior it's filled with poetry in fact The ESS
feels that prose is the medium of poetry which drifts throug
h it as through an ocean in clots of liquid more or less thi
ck translucent jelly sinuous squid awful shark whale so ca
pacious it approaches prose again. And on top of those wate
rs the trusty ESS Broadside cuts the waves sails open to wha
tever wind the winds of circumstance and occasion of pursuit

and evasion never mind the coarse uproar of its prosaic de
cks as tragic Captain Postcard fends off the mailman of fate
to pull alongside the prey grappling hooks poised the firepo
rts explode pointblank with barrages of wordbombs

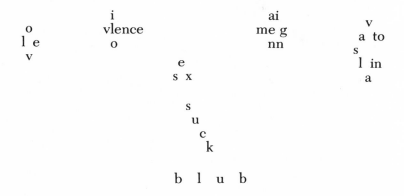

alphabet soup dissolving in the thick warm broth of humanism
fish food again. For as Captain Postcard knows the target
is always poetry. And the bullet is poetry. And the gun is
poetry. Every poem destroys the language a little. Blows a
hunk off the stale intractable block of it. Blows it to bit
s so the fish can eat again and multiply in their many surpr
ising species shapes and hues only to fall prey to bigger f
ish or to fish that are smaller but more numerous and one ho
pes more lively like dull unwieldy epistolary novels that break
down into constituent postcards while tragic Captain Postcar
d sails off his moment past to meet his fate in the bland de
pths of cliche. What you hear is the sound of fish nibbling
alphabets. It's three generations later and all of this has
happened already. Two fishermen with elaborate gear stand o

---

ver a pool and talk about it. They haul out fish one after another club them pull out their guts. When they're done they string them up on their car and take a snapshot. And there it is. The Great American Postcard. They stutter off in the clumsy Model T of analysis bringing home food for thought. Dear ESS. Went fishing today but all I caught was a postcard and it wasn't Serious. Didn't have no Plot. No Charac

FICTION COLLECTIVE
Books in Print

	cloth	paper
The Second Story Man by Mimi Albert	8.95	3.95
Althea by J.M. Alonso	11.95	4.95
Searching for Survivors by Russell Banks	7.95	3.95
Babble by Jonathan Baumbach	8.95	3.95
Chez Charlotte and Emily by Jonathan Baumbach	9.95	4.95
My Father More or Less by Jonathan Baumbach	11.95	5.95
Reruns by Jonathan Baumbach	7.95	3.95
Plane Geometry... by R.M. Berry	12.95	6.95
Heroes and Villains by Jerry Bumpus	12.95	6.95
Things in Place by Jerry Bumpus	8.95	3.95
Ø Null Set by George Chambers	8.95	3.95
The Winnebago Mysteries by Moira Crone	11.95	5.95
Amateur People by Andrée Connors	8.95	3.95
Take It or Leave It by Raymond Federman	11.95	4.95
Coming Close by B.H. Friedman	11.95	5.95
Museum by B.H. Friedman	7.95	3.95
Temporary Sanity by Thomas Glynn	8.95	3.95
Music for a Broken Piano by James Baker Hall	11.95	5.95
The Talking Room by Marianne Hauser	10.95	5.95
Holy Smoke by Fanny Howe	8.95	3.95
In the Middle of Nowhere by Fanny Howe	12.95	6.95
Mole's Pity by Harold Jaffe	8.95	3.95
Mourning Crazy Horse by Harold Jaffe	11.95	5.95
Moving Parts by Steve Katz	8.95	3.95
Stolen Stories by Steve Katz	12.95	6.95
Find Him! by Elaine Kraf	9.95	3.95
The Northwest Passage by Norman Lavers	12.95	6.95
I Smell Esther Williams by Mark Leyner	11.95	5.95
Emergency Exit by Clarence Major	9.95	4.95
Reflex and Bone Structure by Clarence Major	8.95	3.95
Four Roses in Three Acts by Franklin Mason	9.95	4.95
The Secret Table by Mark Mirsky	7.95	3.95
Encores for a Dilettante by Ursule Molinaro	8.95	3.95
Rope Dances by David Porush	8.95	3.95
The Broad Back of the Angel by Leon Rooke	9.95	3.95
The Common Wilderness by Michael Seide	16.95	—
The Comatose Kids by Seymour Simckes	8.95	3.95
Fat People by Carol Sturm Smith	8.95	3.95
Crash-Landing by Peter Spielberg	12.95	6.95
The Hermetic Whore by Peter Spielberg	8.95	3.95
Twiddledum Twaddledum by Peter Spielberg	7.95	3.95
The Endless Short Story by Ronald Sukenick	13.95	6.95
Long Talking Bad Conditions Blues by Ronald Sukenick	9.95	4.95
98.6 by Ronald Sukenick	7.95	3.95
Meningitis by Yuriy Tarnawsky	8.95	3.95
Agnes & Sally by Lewis Warsh	11.95	5.95
Heretical Songs by Curtis White	9.95	4.95
Statements 1	—	3.95
Statements 2	8.95	2.95

Fiction Collective, c/o Dept. of English, Brooklyn College, Brooklyn, NY 11210